"No one has ever run out on me before."

"There's a first time for everything," responded Pagan tartly, trying to pull away from him. His presence did such strange things to her body she could hardly trust herself to stand up.

She felt him draw closer so that the length of his body was beside hers, their hips touching. He tilted her head back; as her eyes closed his lips searched for her own, and then for a long time there was nothing at all but the ecstasy of his touch.

Breathlessly they parted, only to come together again in a swooning delight of pure pleasure.

Then he held her at arm's length. "It isn't only lunch you're hungry for!" he mocked.

His frankness made her blush.

SANDRA CLARK
is also the author of this
Harlequin Romance

2533—MOONLIGHT ENOUGH

Stormy Weather

Sandra Clark

Harlequin Books

TORONTO • NEW YORK • LONDON
AMSTERDAM • PARIS • SYDNEY • HAMBURG
STOCKHOLM • ATHENS • TOKYO • MILAN

Original hardcover edition published in 1983
by Mills & Boon Limited

ISBN 0-373-02569-6

Harlequin Romance first edition September 1983

CHAPTER ONE

PAGAN slithered to a halt, nearly skidding off the rutted track into the rhododendrons which ran down the side of the garden and screened the house from the lane. She backtracked a yard or two so that she could have another look at the sign which had caused her to stop so abruptly, and a look of sheer incredulity spread across her face.

The sign itself wasn't new. It had first appeared a few weeks previously, when the old manor, empty for some two years, its fine gardens gradually becoming choked with weeds and the paint of its white shutters streaked and peeling, had first come on the market. There had been an auction, very well attended, and now it was rumoured that a London businessman had bought the property, some said for a holiday retreat, others for a hotel, or a lakeside restaurant, or, said others, a night club.

Now, however, across the 'sold' sign was another sign about which there could be no speculation.

'Keep Out', it warned emphatically. 'Trespassers will be Prosecuted.' And as if to make sure its message was clearly understood, a new pile of stakes and a coil of barbed wire were heaped beneath it.

Even as Pagan stood there in the rain, re-reading with growing apprehension the warning that she was now encroaching on forbidden territory, a workman came pushing his way through the wet shrubbery with a bag of tools in his hand.

'Excuse me!' she called, dragging her bike towards him.

The man scarcely looked up.

She called again. 'I say, would you mind telling me

what you're doing?' There was an edge to her voice which betrayed her anxiety.

The man put his toolbag down and went over to the pile of stakes. Without doing more than cast a half-glance over his shoulder, he started to pick one of them up.

'Are you fencing off the entrance to the lane?' demanded Pagan incredulously, as if only a spoken testimony would confirm what her eyes were already telling her.

He looked at her blankly through rheumy eyes, as if observing her from a great distance.

'I said, are you fencing off the entrance to the lane?' she asked again, trying to curb the anxiety she couldn't help feeling.

The old man straightened up painfully then. 'Got to be fenced off now, love. Building work starting.'

He took one of the stakes and hammered it with practised ease into the rain-sodden bank at the side of the lane, then he started to line up another one a short distance from the first.

'But how am I to get through if there's barbed wire across the entrance?' she burst out. She pushed a tangle of chestnut hair from her eyes and stood, nonplussed, on the forbidden side of the line of stakes which was now rapidly going up before her gaze. 'How are my pupils supposed to get to the boats?' she demanded. 'There's no other way down to the landing stage!'

'You'll have to ask the mister,' the man threw the muttered words over his shoulder as if plainly embarrassed by her interruption. He plodded on with his work, head bowed, obviously wishing she would go away.

'What mister?' she demanded. 'Who do you mean? Where is he?'

But before the man could reply she was gripping her bike impatiently by the handlebars and was already beginning to push it off down the lane again.

'He's at the house now, is he? This mister, the owner—this London businessman!' Pagan failed to keep the anger out of her voice now, though it was not directed at the old man, who was merely carrying out orders, it seemed.

Not even bothering to get on her bike properly, she scooted it down to the bottom of the lane to the place where it opened out onto a gravel standing where her pupils usually parked their cars.

She couldn't help feeling a tremor of anticipation when she saw the lake suddenly opening out beyond the trees. There was a good stiff breeze this morning and although the rain was coming down in sudden squalls, making the surface of the water change from light to dark, she knew it was going to clear and it would be a good day to be out on the water.

There was no time now to admire the view, nor to question the unexpected presence of a lone windsurfer tacking across the bay. There were more urgent matters to attend to—nothing less than the continued existence of the sailing school itself.

She pushed her bike hastily under the makeshift shelter beside the old dormobile where all the lifejackets were stored, and half running, made off in the direction of the house.

'How dare he!' the words hammered in her head. 'How dare he!' She ran angrily across the straggly uncut grass of the once beautiful lawn. 'How dare he try to fence off our right of way without so much as a warning! London businessman indeed! What does he think I'm going to do? Ferry my pupils over to the jetty in motorboats? Make them paddle?'

She came to a skidding stop and scanned the terrace with troubled eyes. There was a contractor's van round by the side of the house, but the ground floor shutters inside were still across.

Pagan stormed up the stone steps onto the terrace and made for the side of the house where the van was parked. A couple of workmen were unloading materials from the back of it.

Checking herself long enough to control the shaking anger in her voice, she stepped forward and asked them if she could speak to the owner, but even before they both shook their heads, she could tell from the empty sweep of the drive which curved elegantly towards the main road along which she had pedalled so cheerfully not fifteen minutes before that there was no one else around.

The taller of the two, a sandy-haired man in blue overalls, came forward helpfully.

'We're only dropping off a few things on our way to another job,' he told her, 'and then we're tidying up a bit outside, like.'

'You mean you're putting up a barbed-wire fence across my access to the jetty,' Pagan told him warmly. 'I'm trying to run a sailing school down there. How on earth are my pupils supposed to get to the dinghies if there's barbed wire across the end of the lane?'

The man looked uncomfortable. He shrugged. 'All I know is, we've got to make the place secure. There's going to be a lot of equipment lying around here when work gets started come Monday morning.'

'Oh, fine!' she replied sarcastically, unable to help herself. 'So what are my pupils to do over the weekend? I've got sixteen people turning up here tomorrow morning expecting sailing lessons. Am I to tell them to crawl under the wire on their hands and knees, then?'

'I don't know nothing about no sailing school, do you, Jim?' the sandy-haired man nudged his companion.

'He said "drop that stuff off at the Manor," that's all I know.'

'Who said?' Pagan moved a step forward.

'The boss, like. Mr Haynes. Back at the shop.'

'But who told him what to do?' asked Pagan in more conciliatory tones. It was, after all, pointless to get angry with these two, they were only carrying out orders like the old man in the lane.

Neither of them could help. One of them merely repeated, 'We don't know nothing about no sailing school,' and shuffled his feet with discomfiture.

'We're pretty well known round here,' retorted Pagan, piqued to find that they didn't even know of the school's existence, until she caught sight of the lettering on the side of the van. 'But you're not to a local firm, I see. You're over from Kendal way.' She shrugged, for the moment beaten. It was obvious she was wasting her time, and she realised that the two men were probably as mystified as she was by events.

Actually, she thought, kicking a stone as she flung a goodbye at them and began to walk back across the terrace, she wasn't mystified at all. She had half expected something like this. After all, if it was some wealthy outsider used to throwing his weight around who had now taken over at the Manor, he was more than likely to give short shrift to the needs of a little sailing school which just happened to require a continued right of way over his precious land.

'Oh, Uncle!' she thought helplessly. 'If only you'd thought ahead!' She heaved a sigh.

It was through her uncle's lack of foresight that she was in this predicament now, but it was also through her uncle that she had been lucky enough to inherit the school too. And she couldn't blame the poor old love. No one could have guessed that what had started as a hobby to keep a still active ex-nautical man happy would develop into a fully-fledged little business.

In the early days, shortly after her parents died, Pagan had been welcomed into her uncle's lovely house here in the Lake District as if it had been her own home, and at that time the sailing school had been nothing more than a vague dream in her uncle's mind.

Then, one by one, a little fleet of training dinghies

had been built up and Pagan, still a schoolgirl, had begun to help out at weekends and holiday times.

In those days everything had been different. The neighbouring manor house had been full of light and life. It was only when the family had gradually grown up and left one by one that the Colonel, like her uncle, had been left alone.

The two of them would sit yarning together on the terrace every evening, the sailor's glass of rum and the soldier's pink gin ritually seeing down many a sun behind the purple hulk of Ben Ridding.

It had been natural enough for Uncle Henry's old ally to encourage the first informal pupils to use the lane that ran down the side of the Manor between the two properties. It was simply an extension of the sharing over the years between the two old families.

Uncle Henry's lovely house commanded the head of the lake, and the lane, although it seemed to have been originally built for the stables at the back of the Manor, was almost a shared access for them all if they wanted to get down to the lake without going through the grounds themselves. No one had ever thought to query it.

It was only when first the Colonel and then, eighteen months later, Pagan's uncle had died, both men well into their seventies by this time, that questions of change and legal rights had suddenly arisen.

As his only living relative Pagan had automatically inherited the sailing school and the house. What she hadn't known until the will was read out was that most of the boats had been bought by the raising of a second mortgage.

'I'm so very sorry, my dear,' her bank manager had told her, when, still in black and feeling very conscious that she was now entirely alone in the world, she had gone to try to tease some order into the financial affairs she had inherited. 'I'm afraid that in the circumstances I cannot allow the loan to be transferred to you without more security. As you will see, scarcely anything has been paid off. The interest alone. . . .' He spread his hands over the papers on his desk in a gesture of helplessness.

By this time Pagan had had a chance to do some thinking, and she wasn't at all put out. Heavens, she didn't want the millstone of a huge mortgage round her neck. Nor could she envisage living on at the house alone; it was far too large and difficult to run. Soon it would need a lot of expensive work doing to it to bring it up to modern standards, and there was no way she herself could ever afford to take on such a job. She would be glad to have the old place off her hands, sad though it was to have a chapter of her life come to an end.

On the bright side though, now, for the first time in her life, she would be mistress of her own destiny, and she wanted desperately to be free, to test her wings in the outside world.

She had loved her uncle dearly, but through the last few years, though she had never complained, she had felt the increasing responsibility of having to look after an old man. It had weighed more and more heavily upon her, though she hadn't guessed the cause at the time.

Despite the bank manager's forbidding words she smiled quite cheerfully and told him that she intended to sell the house anyway.

'That will put paid to any mortgage, I hope?'

A smile of relief broke across his face. He nodded. 'A very sensible decision, Pagan.'

His use of her first name was due to the fact that he had known her since she had first moved into the house as a gap-toothed twelve-year-old.

'I'm sure you'll also get a very good price for the dinghies too,' he added, shuffling some papers, ready to file them away.

Pagan looked shocked. 'Heavens, I wouldn't think of selling those! They're my livelihood.'

She had the satisfaction of seeing his complacent smile fade for a moment.

'I'm going to run the school myself,' she told him. 'We were just beginning to build up a name for ourselves.'

Modesty stopped her from adding that since she had left sixth-form college she had put such single-minded effort into the business that it was now due almost entirely to her own efforts that Uncle Henry had begun to think of expanding and turning it into a really lucrative little enterprise.

'But—alone?' he queried.

'I have Tim and Jan. They're all for it. Tim says it beats teaching woodwork any day!'

The expression in his eyes told her plainly enough that he thought a pretty young girl of twenty-two wasn't his ideal image of a sailing school proprietor.

Pagan tossed back her thick fall of chestnut hair and her eyes sparkled green with the challenge of it all.

'I've been running the place practically single-handed ever since Uncle Henry's first stroke last summer,' she told him. 'Tim and Jan were very much part-time then. That was the hardest time. This season things should be a lot easier. I intend to convert the old boathouse and live in it. I shall keep a parcel of land round it for a little garden and a winter store for the dinghies. My only grouse is that I shall have no direct access to the jetty itself from the boathouse because of the lie of the garden. However, it's only a short cycle ride round by the main road and down the side lane.'

He had been made fairly speechless by her cut-and-dried manner and though murmuring something about marriage not being the sort of thing to dismiss out of hand in the not too distant future, she had left him wearing an unusually speculative look on his face.

Pagan herself was full of optimism. It was only later

that she had learned that the right of access she had always taken for granted was only a grace and favour right.

At once efforts on the part of her uncle's solicitor had been made to get something more secure established, but it had been impossible to get the trustees of the Colonel's will to commit themselves until the intricacies of the vast estate had been put in some sort of order. After several noncommittal replies to his letters, he had advised her to wait and see what happened when, as was to be hoped, the house finally came up for sale and acquired new owners.

All through her first spring as sole proprietor the dark cloud of uncertainty had hung over the school, and just when she was almost lulled into a feeling that the Colonel's estate would never be straightened out and things would go on for ever as they were, up had gone the 'For Sale' signs and in a few short weeks the whole existence of the school had come openly into question.

Pagan thrust her clenched up fists deep into the wide pockets of her petrol blue oilskin. She had flung it on over a pair of jeans and a white lambswool polo-neck sweater after a hurried glance at the weather from her bedroom window that morning, and now her grey-green eyes were as stormy as the lake itself, and her generously wide mouth had lost its usual upward smiling curve and was set in a fierce line of determination.

Rain pattered in little showers and sudden squalls on her oilskin, and showered her chestnut hair with a fine spray which turned it an even darker hue. It had started to curl in little tendrils around her face as she paced angrily towards the line of tarpaulin-covered dinghies. Her canary yellow sailing boots with the white tie tops seemed to be the only bright spot in the unbroken haze of rain-drenched shoreline.

As she walked her thoughts teemed confusedly in her head. She was supposed to be checking a new jib strop

for one of the dinghies before the weekend pupils
turned up in the morning, but now, with all this, was
there any point?

She should have made greater efforts to establish her
rights, instead of allowing herself to be lulled in a false
sense of fair play. As if it was realistic to expect a
businessman to play fair!

He could so easily have warned her that he was going
to play it strictly by the book, fencing off every square
inch of his property like this!

If the darned stuff wasn't removed by the morning
she would have to take the law into her own hands and
hang the consequences. She couldn't allow her pupils to
be turned away by these Gestapo methods.

Her shoulders squared. She had never been afraid of
confrontations and she wasn't going to lose her cool
now. This man, whoever he was, would have to be
reasonable and give the solicitors time to sort
something out.

Across the rain-dark lake the windsurfer was tacking
back and forth in melancholy isolation, and as she
approached the lines of boats, the familiar, regular
tapping of the halyards against the aluminium masts
seemed only to accentuate the increasing gloom of the
scene.

Her shoulders tightened with anger. She would jolly
well cut down the barbed wire herself if it wasn't
removed by morning. She wasn't afraid—not she!

But, whispered the voice of caution, what good
would it do to get on the wrong side of this man,
whoever he was, right from the very first? She was
going to have to play the whole game very carefully in
order to convince him that the school, well run and
orderly, was not going to create a nuisance on his land.

For a split second Pagan had almost felt like giving
up the whole thing. But she was struck by the grace and
beauty of the red, white and blue sail out in the lake
and knew with a surge of pleasure that she would never

be happy in a dull office job while there was a chance of tasting the joy and excitement of being on the water and being her own boss.

At once her fighting spirit took over and she marched resolutely towards the row of boats neatly lined up on the shingle. It was a simple job to replace the old jib strop with the new one, and as she worked she made up her mind what she would do.

So absorbed was she in her thoughts that she was unaware of anyone's presence until she heard the scrunch of approaching footsteps on the shingle and a pleasant masculine voice called out, 'Hi there!'

She spun round with surprise to find that the windsurfer had silently come into land and was now loping the last few yards up the shingle. When he drew level he stopped and grinned self-confidently down, amused at her evident confusion.

Slowly Pagan drew herself up. Just because he had caught her unawares there was no reason for him to look so pleased with himself!

She found herself looking into a pair of the clearest, brightest eyes she had ever seen, so light a blue they were almost the same shade as bottle glass which has been washed smooth and opaque by the continual action of the sea, yet bright when he smiled as he was doing now, diamond-bright.

'H-hi!' she stammered, trying to pull herself together. Avoiding his glance, she looked back at the sailboard. Its neat triangle was now laid flat on the beach where he had pulled it up above the waterline. It was rare to find a windsurfer as far down the lake as this. Boards were for hire at the other end, an almost impossible distance to sail. Perhaps he had hired it from one of the less distant hotels, or perhaps it was even his own, and he had launched it from one of the coves which were easily accessible from the main road. It was no trouble to carry a board like that on top of a car.

Pagan let her glance come back to rest on him in an

appraising sort of way. He was certainly worth appraising. Tall, tough, blond and muscular, he hadn't a spare ounce of flesh on him. He was all solid muscle, and bronzed too, as if he had spent long months in the sun.

He was wearing a pair of scruffy cut-down jeans, very short on the thigh as if to draw attention to their hard muscularity, and a T-shirt which did the same job for his biceps. His tanned feet, unusually long and well-shaped for a man, were thrust into an old pair of blue rubber flip-flops.

Pagan felt overpowered with the sense of his sheer strength and physical fitness. But his face drew her glance, for it was even more compelling, with its tanned, hawklike features, high cheekbones, fine blond eyebrows hooding eyes of that exotic colour, and finally, the thick, wavy blond hair, too long, she thought, for respectability, and bleached almost silver by the sun so that it made an outrageous contrast with the gleaming dark tan of his skin.

His eyes glittered again as if sparked by jets of silver as he returned her blatant inspection of him with a quizzical half-smile. With a start she pulled herself together.

To cover her confusion, she said sharply, 'I suppose you know you're trespassing?'

His grin widened to reveal a flash of small perfectly even teeth.

'Am I? I didn't know.'

His ease and nonchalance stung her to a quick retort.

'You know now,' she said. 'This is a private sailing school. I don't like unauthorised people landing here. It gets in the way of the pupils.'

'Pupils?' he grinned, making a show of sweeping the deserted beach and the offshore water with his strange, lively eyes. 'I see no sign of pupils.'

'You will do,' replied Pagan, 'assuming you're around long enough. Now would you mind leaving?'

A flicker of surprise showed itself in the man's eyes, but the glitter came back to them almost immediately.

'Why should I?' he asked easily, not budging.

Pagan felt an overwhelming urge to get rid of this man as soon as possible. There was something dangerously disconcerting about him, something she felt she could not handle, and trouble was the last thing she wanted at the moment.

'You're rather territorial,' he rejoined after a pause during which his amused glance had lazily raked her from head to foot.

'Look, I'll tell you why—because it's private property, that's why,' she began heatedly, then in a more conciliatory tone, 'I can't guess where you've come from but the last thing I want is an army of hooray-harrys sailboarding all over the bay, confusing the learners and creating havoc with all and sundry. The lake's big enough for everybody if we all keep to our own patch.'

By 'all and sundry' she meant her new neighbour, but she wasn't going to tell him that.

'Do I look like a hooray-harry?' he asked in mockingly exaggerated surprise. He tried to put a hurt look momentarily on to the clean-cut lines of his face before breaking into an irresistible grin.

Pagan blushed, annoying herself by such an irrelevant show of emotion, and pushed the tangle of chestnut hair from her forehead in an action that habitually betrayed uncertainty.

'Not you personally, perhaps,' she conceded, 'but sailboarders always seem to have armies of usually drunken friends in tow——' She tailed off weakly. He was looking at her in such a way she felt her breath tighten in her throat. To mask her confusion she added, 'I'm busy now. I have to get on.'

She turned her back on him, pointedly showing him he was in the way. And as if to get the message home to him she warned, 'The weather's going to blow up pretty soon. You'll find it hard work sailing back up the lake then.' And when she shot a look over her shoulder to find that he still hadn't budged, she added, 'Just because this is a lake people seem to think it's quite safe, but it can be treacherous when the wind gets up because of the mountains on either side.'

'I expect it's very deep and dark, too, with all kinds of ugly man-eating monsters lurking at the bottom just waiting for careless windsurfers to fall into their mouths. . . .'

'Oh, for goodness' sake——!' Pagan burst out.

He was laughing openly. His skin crinkled at the corners of his eyes and two deep laugh lines grooved on either side of his mouth. His laughter was so infectious she almost joined in, but she checked herself in time. There was no point in encouraging him, and besides, he *was* laughing at her authority and mocking her warning about the dangers of the lake.

'Don't expect *me* to come and fish you out,' she told him shortly.

She wished he would just sail quietly away. She didn't like to walk off, leaving him here with the boats. Not because she didn't trust him, instinctively she knew he was all right, but because it was her property, and to walk off and leave him here was somehow to concede something to him. So she stood her ground and for a moment their eyes held before he asked lightly.

'So you're a sailing instructor?'

Pagan felt confused by the teasing note in his voice.

'I'm the owner,' she replied curtly.

He pretended to look astonished.

Here it comes, she thought, the line about, what's a slip of a girl like you doing running a school like this, but instead he said, 'It sounds fascinating. Do you teach all levels?'

Because he looked genuinely interested she couldn't stop herself.

'We do all the RYA grades,' she told him. 'That's the

Royal Yachting Association,' she explained when he seemed to raise his eyebrows as if for some explanation of the letters.

'It looks like an ideal place for beginners,' he returned, 'except, of course, when the wind really gets up.' He grinned lopsidedly.

'You may scoff,' she burst out, 'but it's not as safe as it looks. I have to be very careful with the youngsters.'

'Teach children too?'

'School parties, families, yes. I'd like to run summer schools for children so that they could come along without their parents. They seem to learn quicker that way.'

She began to warm to the subject, but checked herself in time. Who did he think he was, trying to draw her out like this? She'd heard another school was going to open up last year, no doubt having seen the success she and her uncle were having, but eventually nothing had come of it. People had warned her though to watch out for competition.

'You've got to play things close to your chest in this game,' Tim had warned.

The stranger's gaze swept the neat line of boats admiringly.

'To handle all this by yourself,' he murmured, 'that's quite a job for anyone your age.'

'Not entirely alone,' she couldn't help smiling. 'I couldn't allow absolute beginners out in the boats by themselves. Apart from the risk to themselves, they're expensive craft.'

She smiled again. Obviously the man, for all his self-confidence and expertise with the sailboard, knew next to nothing about sailing.

'It's not like windsurfing,' she told him by way of explanation. 'I can't just give a pupil five minute's land drill, hand them a wet-suit and a boat and tell them to get on with it—which is what, I gather, happens when most people learn to windsurf. They have to go out with an instructor for several hours in different weather conditions and answer a lot of theoretical questions before they're competent to handle a dinghy safely by themselves.'

She had the satisfaction of seeing a respectful look come into the stranger's face.

'I'd no idea it was so difficult,' he told her. 'It looks so easy, doesn't it? You do the actual teaching yourself, then?'

'Yes, some of it. That's the best part. But I'm lucky— I've got a man and his wife who've been with the school almost since the beginning, and every summer in the height of the season I take on several students who work through the vacation for me.'

'Students?' he queried.

'All properly qualified instructors, of course,' she added quickly.

'Of course,' he nodded, his eyes serious. 'You must be very talented to be able to handle all the organisation of a business like this as well as being yourself a competent sailor,' he told her solemnly.

Pagan shot him a keen glance. There was something about the glimmer in his eyes almost as if he was—but no, his expression was politely straight-faced, and there was no sign of ill-concealed mockery in his voice.

He went on, 'Don't you find all this takes up a lot of time? When do you have time to go out and enjoy yourself?'

'My work is my enjoyment,' she told him shortly.

Stranger though he was, he had touched a chord. Through the years of late adolescence when other girls were going out with boys and experimenting with make-up and fashion, Pagan had been tied to the house, looking after Uncle Henry and spending all her spare hours running the school.

It seemed to her sometimes that she had missed out on all the fun of being a teenager. And now, here she was, twenty-two, with the irresponsibility of those years forever denied to her.

In fact, it was only since Uncle Henry's death, when she had at last been able to take stock of her life, that she had actually started to think about less serious things, such as buying clothes for fun rather than practicality. Faynia had guided her in the right direction there.

Good old Faynia, an old school friend and now owner of a small but successful boutique in Windermere, she was honest to the point of rudeness when it came to selling clothes.

'It's no good sending someone out of here looking like a freak,' she told Pagan. 'I've my name to think of.'

And certainly Pagan had been stopped from making one or two expensively garish mistakes in the early days, before her natural good taste had had a chance to assert itself.

All this flashed through her mind now as she looked at the blond stranger standing in front of her. He looked as if he had never known responsibility. He looked as if he would fight every inch of the way at the thought of giving up an inch of freedom. He carried his independence like a banner.

'These sailing bums,' she thought, 'they're all alike. They move on from place to place exactly as the fancy takes them.' It seemed vaguely reprehensible. On the other hand, she could quite see the attraction of a life like that.

She smiled wistfully and he returned her glance with a disappointed shrug.

'All work and no play?' There was a mocking lift to his finely drawn eyebrows. He regarded her quizzically for a moment before speaking. Then he shrugged. 'Here am I, a stranger to the district, hoping to discover a little night-life to alleviate my loneliness. . . .' He paused. 'Perhaps we can help each other to discover where the action is?'

Pagan coloured violently. A pass was the last thing she'd expected just now, her mind full of worries as it was, and coming from a man such as this—so virile, so obviously self-reliant, so *free*-looking. She couldn't imagine him being anywhere but automatically in the thick of action, nor short of a glamorous girl-friend or two with which to share it. He must be trying to make a fool of her.

She drew back, her eyes steely.

'I'm in rather a hurry this morning, so I'd be most grateful if you'd get off my property now. I don't intend to waste all morning patrolling the shore to keep people off. If you're seen to land here it'll attract others like bees round a honey-pot——' She broke off in confusion. Her words had unexpectedly acquired an overtone she hadn't intended. 'I mean—everybody'll think they have a right to land here.'

She turned away, angry with herself, angry at the tell tale flush on her cheeks.

All right, she would admit it. He was damned attractive. The trouble was, the man knew it. No doubt he thought her a simple-minded local yokel who would jump at the chance of a date with a passing stranger, no matter how disreputable-looking.

She pulled the tarpaulin back to cover the boat up, then she started to make her way to the lean-to where she'd left her bike.

He was still watching her as if expecting an answer, and she threw him a look of chagrin.

'There are plenty of bars in the hotels, I suppose,' she felt constrained to tell him. 'Some of the more up-to-date ones even have discos at the weekends. But there's nothing much else. You'll just have to ask around.'

She paused but couldn't help adding primly, 'People come here to do hill-walking, or to sail. They're not usually in a fit state to do anything much else come nightfall.'

She coloured again at the unconscious meaning which could be read into her innocent words. A meaning he had undoubtedly read, for his eyes were dancing with devilment.

'You'll just have to suffer some rather boring evenings,' she finished weakly.

He laughed aloud. 'That's the last thing I intend to do! I'm no puritan. And I don't believe suffering is necessarily good for one's soul. On the contrary——' he took a step forward, 'I think any form of suffering is positively bad, don't you?'

Pagan smiled despite herself.

'You'd make a rotten sailor, then,' she told him. 'It's jolly uncomfortable much of the time. You'd be strictly a light airs man.'

His face broke into a craggy smile. 'Light airs?'

'You only go out when the wind isn't above a whisper and the temperature is somewhere in the eighties. Like my chief instructor, if he had a choice.'

The stranger shook his blond head and his voice was soft. 'Oh no, I didn't say I didn't like a challenge. I'm willing to put up with quite some discomfort if the prize is worth it.'

His strangely compelling eyes held her as if deliberately. Once again Pagan turned away in angry confusion at the suggestive tone in his voice.

If she asked him to go again and he refused, there was going to be nothing else she could do about it. Except lose face.

She felt helpless suddenly. She felt like putting her foot slap bang through his sail where it lay half across the narrow streamlined board and the gravel shore.

She could damage his boat in a minute. That would teach him to come trespassing!

Surprised, herself, at the strength of her reaction, she made her way towards the lean-to where she had left her bike and dragged it from under the shelter with a dark look.

She was pleased to see the man was now making his way back to his sailboard. She watched him out of the corners of her eyes as he pulled the narrow board into the water. He stood with one foot on it to control it and one foot in the water, his hands gripping the slim mast, but before he raised it right up, he called to her with insolent cheerfulness.

'Do I take it I'm being given the brush-off?'

'Take it any way you like,' she replied curtly. 'I haven't time to stand around gossiping all day like you.'

'What makes you think I have time either? I may be working now,' he added unexpectedly.

'What?' She stopped dead.

He regarded her with a poker face.

'Perhaps I'm a professional windsurfer,' he explained experimentally.

'Perhaps you're an astronaut too,' she retorted. 'I still haven't time to stand around all day.'

With that she started to push her bike off again. When she got to the lane end she glanced quickly back over her shoulder. He was still standing there with the water lapping round his ankles.

'Aren't you going to teach me to sail?' he asked, as a parting shot.

Pagan looked back at his scruffy shorts and T-shirt.

'I doubt whether you could afford the fees,' she retorted.

With a toss of her head she turned her back on him and scooted a few yards up to the top of the lane. There she paused for a moment to make sure he was really going.

He had lifted the long mast upright now and the wind was snatching fitfully at it. He swivelled it into the wind so that the sail flapped uselessly for a moment.

'Book me a lesson first thing in the morning,' he shouted.

'I'll do that,' she replied ironically. 'Nine o'clock sharp!'

With one movement he had pushed off from the shore, turned the sail to catch the wind, and was in a moment off the shore and making way, back along the lake.

He had time to raise one hand in a nonchalant farewell, before the wind strengthened and took him speeding away.

'He should be wearing a wet-suit,' thought Pagan critically as she saw him having to lie far out over the water to keep the sail vertical.

Soon it was nothing more than a speck in the middle of the lake.

CHAPTER TWO

'HOLIDAYMAKERS, huh! No sense, any of them.' Pagan sipped her coffee. 'They don't realise it's too early in the year for the water to have had time to warm up properly. Ten minutes in there and they're exposing themselves to the risk of hypothermia. It's no laughing matter!'

'You shouldn't worry, he's not your responsibility,' replied Faynia with a small smile.

She and Pagan were sitting in the comfortable little cubbyhole at the back of the shop where Faynia brewed coffee and read magazines when trade was slack. The sound of a lively beat number drifted through from the shop and one or two lunchtime shoppers were browsing through the clothes. Faynia was keeping one eye on the shop while still managing to give her attention to Pagan.

But now she muttered, 'If that fat trollop dares to try on that blue I'll murder her, so help me! Honestly, Pagan, I think some of them are colour-blind. Now you—you'd look fantastic in it, with your colouring.' She shot a look at the girl sitting opposite. 'Do you want me to try to rescue it before she gets her hands on it and starts in on the zip?'

Pagan giggled, 'You are dreadful, Faynia!'

In reply Faynia uncoiled lazily from the depths of her armchair and moved slinkily into the shop.

Already tall, with her dark hair coiled in a casual knot on top of her head and wearing strappy high-heeled sandals, she towered over the potential customer, but her manner exuded nothing but a desire to offer every assistance.

Pagan was sent into suppressed giggles again. Faynia,

however, straight-faced, and, indeed, with uncanny perception, brought out one or two dresses which were far more suitable for the rather plump brunette who had been looking longingly at the blue dress. This was now whipped away, and Pagan found herself holding the diaphanous bundle in her arms while Faynia pushed her firmly towards the changing room.

'At least try it on and do me the favour of keeping it away from her. She's just the type to insist on buying it if she thinks I'm keeping it from her,' she hissed.

Pagan had no choice but to do as Faynia asked—not that she wanted to resist. It was exactly her sort of dress, and she had been keeping a covetous eye on it ever since it came in.

She slipped into the changing room. The dress went on easily over her head and she paused to admire the transformation it seemed to make. With no make-up her face looked pale, so that she seemed younger than she was, and her rich hair gave her a piquant look. The dress, however, drew attention to all the right places, and for a moment she was surprised at how voluptuously feminine she appeared. She had become so used to seeing herself in jeans and sailing sweater that she hadn't realised that she could, if she tried, look one hundred per cent female.

She came out into the shop to show Faynia.

'O.K.,' her friend commented laconically, perching herself on her stool behind the counter and yawning. 'So what? I knew it was you.'

'Thanks for letting me try it on,' said Pagan, not at all put out by Faynia's apparent lack of enthusiasm. She knew her of old. She began to unfasten it. 'It's just beautiful, but where would *I* ever wear a dress like this?' She signed. 'I'd love an excuse to get it!'

Faynia eyed her with detached amusement. 'Well now,' she said, her eyes lively with humour, 'You've just spent fifteen minutes telling me about some gorgeous blond hunk of a windsurfer. So who knows?'

'It was *not* fifteen minutes! And I didn't call him a gorgeous blond hunk——' broke in Pagan heatedly.

Faynia laughed lazily. 'You didn't use those exact words,' she agreed, 'but I'm sure if you'd thought of them first you would have.'

'You're terrible!' Pagan managed a weak smile. 'I was merely sounding off about the trials and tribulations of running a sailing school, simply looking for a bit of sympathy, not trying to get myself paired off with the first passing stranger of the season. Sailing bums,' she shrugged, 'they're ten a penny.'

Faynia threw her head back in a throaty laugh.

'All I can say, darling, is it's about time you stopped being so choosy. You're going to finish up an old maid at this rate—and,' she added unexpectedly, 'if you're thinking of making any changes, you won't necessarily have to twist my arm to get me to let you have that rag at cost should you ever find the need to look a million dollars. O.K.?'

Pagan couldn't help breaking into a wide smile.

'You're not a bad old stick underneath,' she teased, 'despite your eccentric sales technique!'

She went back into the changing room to don reluctantly enough her òld jeans again. When she emerged, the brunette was writing a cheque for both of the dresses Faynia had shown her.

'Eccentric but effective,' murmured Faynia as she rang in the cheques. 'Now then, tell me what your dishy Mr Tebbit had to say to you just now,' she turned expectantly to her friend when the customer had gone.

When Pagan had reached home again later that morning she had rung the contractors in Kendal to try to find out who had authorised them to put barbed wire across the lane end, but they had only been able to give her the name of a firm of solicitors in town who were acting for the new owners. Unsure what to do next, Pagan had rung her own solicitor—that was, the firm with whom her uncle had always dealt.

The elder partner, now retired, had been one of his closest friends, but his own son had long since taken over the firm's practice. Since her uncle's death, Pagan had inevitably had quite a lot to do with them, and Mr Tebbit Senior, the son of her uncle's friend, that was, had taken an avuncular interest in her doings.

His own son had recently joined the firm, following in his grandfather's and his father's footsteps. His interest in Pagan's affairs, however, could not by any means have been described as avuncular. Dishy he was too, as Faynia so succinctly put it, but in a rumpled, boyish sort of way, and Faynia never lost an opportunity to point out how appealing he was.

Now, at her reference to John, Pagan grinned.

'I just might need that blue dress. If I play my cards right I think there's a Hunt Ball coming up.' She wrinkled her nose. 'Sounds a bit of a bore, though, doesn't it? All those horsey types en masse?' She shrugged. 'Anyway, when I told him about the barbed wire he got quite cross—for him!'

'I like placid men,' Faynia paused. 'Some of the time at least!' She laughed. 'Less trouble than the more volatile sort. However, go on.'

'I was hoping you'd let me.' Pagan took a deep breath. 'Well, he rang their solicitors for me, all ready for a showdown, but the man who deals with it was in Court and I was just about to leave, having finished my coffee and noticing that John was beginning to cast anxious looks towards his father's office when——'

'Do you think he's scared of his father?' broke in Faynia. 'That's a bad sign.'

'How should I know?—oh, *do* let me get on,' said Pagan in exasperation.

'I won't utter another word,' retorted Faynia.

'Well, as I was saying, I was just on the point of leaving when the phone rang and it was the other solicitors saying that Mr de Laszlo, that's the new owner, was at present in the area and would we ring his secretary to arrange a meeting at our earliest.'

'Good. Progress at last,' said Faynia. 'So what are you looking so weird about?'

Pagan shot a glance in the full-length mirror. 'Do I look weird? I look quite normal to me.'

'You've got that gleam of battle in your eye. It reminds me of the time you had that crackbrained idea to have a bash at the Transatlantic Yacht Race.'

Pagan pulled a face. 'Don't think you've heard the last of that! All I need is a sponsor.'

'And a yacht.'

'Thanks for the encouragement!'

'Any time,' shrugged Faynia.

'I can see you want to get back to selling this overpriced junk to hard-up housewives, so I'll leave you to it——'

'Hang about,' said Faynia, jumping up. 'There *is* something else, isn't there?'

A flutter of apprehension made Pagan bite her lip for a moment. She gave Faynia a sideways look.

'It's only that he must be absolutely loaded,' she said in a small, awed voice. 'I'm to meet him at his hotel——' She paused, then she named the most exclusive hotel on the lake and watched Faynia's predictable reaction.

'Not bad,' murmured Faynia with approval.

'Yes, but——' Pagan paused again, then she said, 'It's not as if he's only booked a room for a few nights. . . . He's got a whole suite—for an indefinite period!'

She had the satisfaction of seeing Faynia for once open-mouthed.

'How do you know all this?' she quizzed eventually.

'I happen to know a girl on the switchboard. You know her too. We were at school together, until the fifth year. Remember Ann Gordon?'

For a moment Faynia smiled. 'Good old Annie! I wondered where she'd ended up.' Then her face took on the hard, practical look she had when she was doing her books or planning her next season's sales drive. 'Why would he want a relatively small place like the Manor, then?' she demanded.

'Small?' gulped Pagan.

'By his apparent standards, nothing more than a pied-à-terre!'

'Maybe he thinks small is beautiful?'

'With a bank account that size?' Faynia quipped.

'What I'm worried about is how he's going to regard us—I mean, the School. What's he going to think about having a sailing school on his boundary?'

Faynia's face held a look of concern which she tried quickly to hide. 'When do you meet this Laszlo man, then?'

'Monday morning, ten-thirty.'

'And I suppose you're planning to turn up in gumboots and jeans?'

'I hadn't really thought——'

'I didn't think you had. Wait here.' Faynia got up and went to the stockroom. When she emerged she held a suit, still in its cellophane wrapper. 'Come on, no arguing. It's a loan. And I know it's your size, so get in there. It's time to put on your battledress!'

Once again she was pushing Pagan towards the changing room, and with a little flicker of pleasure Pagan let her hands nestle in the luxurious softness of the Liberty print wool suit which Faynia was so insistently thrusting into her arms.

Next morning Pagan leapt out of bed with an unexpected sense of anticipation. She whizzed in and out of the shower, briskly donned an oatmeal-coloured hand-knitted sailing sweater and a pair of slim-fitting blue jeans which drew attention to the long slim length of her legs, then, still barefooted, she brushed her hair vigorously until it shone.

She spent rather longer than usual tying it back in a

neat ribbon, then she took the unusual step of applying a little discreet make-up to draw attention to her large, dark-lashed green eyes.

'I'll do,' she thought, inspecting herself critically in the long mirror on her dressing-room wall, then she thrust her feet into a pair of thick socks and went downstairs into the little kitchen to fix herself some breakfast. While she was brewing coffee and heating up a couple of croissants she tried to discover the reason for her sudden sense of exhilaration.

It was, admittedly, the first weekend of the season. That was exciting in itself. It was true, too, that the problem of the barbed wire had been solved most satisfactorily the previous night by the simple expedient of reliable old Tim coming along on his bike and lifting the stakes out of the ground and placing them in a neat pile under the rhododendrons at the side of the lane.

He had looked quite pleased with himself by the time he had finished, and he rejoined his wife and Pagan at the boathouse with much rubbing of the hands at a job well done. Pagan had made them all a cup of coffee, and added a dash of rum to each cup, as there was a feeling that they were celebrating something.

Jan had raised her coffee cup with a smile. 'Here's to the new season, Pagan. May the school and all of us flourish.'

'May our enemies be confounded,' added Tim, sleeking his beard down with the palm of his hand in a familiar gesture.

They had all parted in good spirits after that, and Pagan had gone to bed feeling less worried than she thought she had any right to expect. But it was underneath all this that she still felt a bubbly kind of happiness whose source was difficult to discover.

She took her breakfast to the large L-shaped sitting-room so that she could look out over the lake, and once or twice, while she munched her muesli waiting for the coffee to perk, she felt her glance sweep the lake as if searching for something.

The lake was of course empty at this time of the morning, and although she scanned it casually from side to side there was no glimpse of any sail in sight. The unbroken sheet of pale blue winked back in the sunlight, concealing nothing.

Pagan sighed and stretched. It was still early, but she might as well get herself down there and start preparing the boats. Recently she had been reluctant to leave the boathouse in the morning. Somehow she had managed to create just the right atmosphere of cosiness and functional elegance. It made her want to linger over her books and she had had to make a real effort to tear herself away.

To call it the boathouse was something of a misnomer now as of course no boats were stored there and it had been turned into an enviably picturesque little two-bedroomed house. Its upper floor actually jutted out over the lake, and Pagan had made this top room into a spacious bedroom for herself.

In one corner was a miniature study, a small desk cubbyholed amidst the bookshelves. A portable typewriter sat amidst the orderly chaos and bright red filing cabinets fitted discreetly within the work area. She had tried to retain the natural stone features of the original boathouse, only adding double-glazed french windows along one wall. These led on to the white-painted balcony which had already been a feature of the original Edwardian building, and as they faced east over the lake, they afforded spectacular views of the rising sun between Brath Rigg and Long Fell. There was a spare room at the back, on the land side, for any visiting friends, and an attractive mirrored bathroom with a shower cubicle between the two rooms.

The corresponding accommodation below consisted of a comfortable kitchen-dining room, utility room and the L-shaped living room, so that once again fullest advantage could be taken of the splendid views across the lake to the mountains beyond.

Pagan had taken her time over the furnishings, being unused to the practicalities of home-making, but Faynia had shown her where the most stylish furnishing fabrics were to be bought and together with the bits and pieces bequeathed to her from her uncle's many sailing trips abroad she had been able to take her time over the winter months when the sailing school was closed in making the place as attractive as possible.

Unknown to anyone else, now that she had a base from which to work, her thoughts had begun to stray in quite another direction. Faynia had hit on it yesterday when she mentioned the Transatlantic Yacht Race. Little did she know how many evenings Pagan would sit up late at her work-bench upstairs, poring over navigation manuals, learning all she could about the race from the accounts written up by successful participants of previous years.

Sometimes she thought Faynia was right. She was mad. It was a crazy idea. Other times she felt the excitement of it fill her whole being so that she knew she would never forgive herself if she didn't at least have a shot at it.

Finance was the big bugbear, she well knew, and she had started on a campaign to find sponsorship for her attempt. So far there had been several polite refusals, but recently she had been asked to give more detailed information other than that contained in her preliminary letters of enquiry, and she hoped it would only be a question of time now before someone finally said yes.

She knew her uncle would have approved, as they had often talked about it together before his death. He had made the stories of his own sailing exploits come vibrantly alive and Pagan knew she had been entirely seduced by the siren song of his yarns.

Somehow it hadn't seemed so crazy when he had been alive. It only seemed so now when she drove into

Kendal or Ambleside to do the weekly shopping and saw all the local townspeople going about their daily business in such a settled, timeless sort of way. Year by year, generation by generation even, nothing much seemed to change, and she often thought of John and his family with a curious, incredulous fascination.

Wanderlust seemed to be a feeling entirely alien to his nature. Pagan thought often about that. Needless to say, she had never mentioned the Transatlantic Race to him.

Now she shrugged briskly into her reefer jacket, chose a navy blue headscarf with a scarlet pattern round the edge just in case the wind really blew up, and made for the outdoors.

Just before leaving she looked round once with satisfaction. It *was* good to have a place of one's own. Full of the warmth of well-being, she locked the door and pocketed the key. But it was towards the sound of the wind stiffening the sails and making the halyards crack against the masts that her steps were ineluctably leading her.

The morning passed swiftly. But for some reason she felt strangely deflated. Not that everything hadn't gone well enough.

Jan had had a slight problem but a minor one with one of her pupils, but then there was always some fourteen-year-old boy who thought he knew it all—a fledgling man testing his wings for a lifetime of ruling the roost, thought Pagan ironically. She sighed and gave a last glance along the beach.

Tim and Jan were wheeling their bikes towards the lane. Tim gave her a cheery thumbs-up sign and she waved back to indicate that she would see them tomorrow.

She had half promised to meet John and some of his friends in a hotel further down the lake later on. Faynia was coming too, being between boy-friends, and she was talking about a pub which had just been re-opened with a new restaurant and dance band.

If I can drag myself out tonight there promises to be a pleasant time ahead, Pagan thought, with illogical gloom.

She shook herself. She wasn't a fool and she knew the cause for her present despondency. She mocked herself for being so gullible. A joking enquiry about sailing lessons was just that, a joke. And she had been stupid enough to take him seriously!

She began to walk back up the shingle. It was a good job he hadn't shown up, for all the boats were fully booked. And she couldn't imagine a great hulking giant like that spending the day squashed in a little dinghy with three or four other people. He'd be the type to have the boat over as soon as set foot in it, she thought, wheeling her bike towards the lane.

She turned round to have one last look at the now empty lake, then her eyes widened. A hand seemed to take hold of her inside somewhere around the heart and give it a slow squeeze.

She watched the red, white and blue triangle, looking very small in the distance, edge bit by bit round the headland from the far end of the lake. It was coming on a broad reach and making good progress towards the small island in the middle. Pagan watched as it tacked back and forth towards the shore. It was difficult to see who was sailing it, but there was no doubt that he was now sailing as close to the wind as he could. She watched, hardly breathing, till the bright fair hair and bronze limbs left no doubt as to the identity of the man standing aboard. There could be no two like that.

Pagan rested her bike against a tree and walked slowly down to the water's edge. There was no doubt about it now, he was definitely heading for the landing stage. She waited with tightly clenched hands.

Soon he was within hailing distance. The next minute a strong wind brought his board scraping up in a welter of loose sail on to the shingle.

'Permission to land, ma'am?' he asked before stepping down.

'If I said no would you go back out again?' she asked drily.

'Do you want to try me?' He paused, balancing with practised ease on the beached sailboard.

Pagan thrust both hands into the pockets of her reefer jacket and regarded him with an amused look. The wind trailed its fingers sinuously through her tangle of chestnut hair and she wondered if he could hear the sound of her heart beating as loudly as she herself.

He let the mast drop down, half in and half out of the water, leaving it there as he strode athletically over the shingle towards her.

Pagan tried to school her features into an indifferent mask, afraid that he might notice her sudden urge to smile. But when he drew level he was smiling too.

'I hope you're not going to tick me off for missing my sailing lesson this morning?' he began.

'Oh, it's all right—I'll just charge it to your account,' she replied nonchalantly. 'I expect you overslept.'

'Yes. It's some night-life you've got around here. I didn't get to bed until ten-thirty!'

He was standing needlessly close, so it seemed, and Pagan edged away a little. She had momentarily forgotten just how tall he was and also how indecently fit he seemed.

'You've relaxed your vendetta against trespassers, then?' he teased, his lean face crinkling attractively into a smile.

'Trespassers? Don't talk to me about trespassers!' burst out Pagan before she could stop herself. 'They and I are on one side.' She had a sudden urge to tell him about her worries of the previous day and the little triumph with the barbed wire. His raised eyebrows seemed to be an invitation, so she added, 'I'm afraid I'm going to be trespassing in order to get back home tonight. The fascist who's just bought the property over there,' she nodded towards the Manor, 'happens to own our right of access. He had the cheek to try to fence the lane off yesterday, so we had to creep out at dead of night to do a little vandalism. That'll show him!' she grinned. 'So we're all trespassers now.'

'He had it fenced off?' He looked puzzled.

She shrugged. 'Marvellous, isn't it? The things some people will do!'

He seemed thoughtful for a moment, but the bronzed levels of his face told her nothing.

'I was jolly mad when I found out,' Pagan went on.

'I can see that,' he replied solemnly. 'Have you tried to tell him how you feel about all this?'

Pagan threw her head back with a scornful laugh. 'You must be joking! What do you think a man like that is going to say to me? I mean, he's absolutely loaded!' She looked at his scruffy cut-down jeans without being able to help herself. With an effort she dragged her eyes back to the man's compelling gaze. 'He'll take one look at the sailing school and laugh his head off. We're just peanuts to him. I mean, what could possibly be in it for someone like that? A flashy property tycoon or whatever he's supposed to be. He'll try to give us short shrift, but he's certainly going to have a fight on his hands if he starts his fascist strong-arm tactics with me!' Her eyes shone green with the challenge.

'What makes you think he's a property tycoon?' he asked.

'People talk, don't they?'

'Do they?' He hesitated. 'What else do they say?'

'Not much. He's keeping a low profile. He probably finds it easier to hire minions to do his dirty work rather than do it himself.'

'Dirty work?' He looked stern.

'Like forcing my sailing school to close,' retorted Pagan, bunching her fists.

'I'm sure it won't come to that.' He looked firm.

'No, it jolly well won't if I have anything to do with it. But that's what he'll try. It stands to reason, doesn't it? We're no *use* to him. And from his point of view we'll merely be a nuisance, driving down the side of his property a couple of times a day.'

'Only at weekends, though. If you tell him that——'

'And through the week in the summer. I run some weekly courses too. I'm planning to expand those. But of course,' she scowled, 'if this dreadful man starts being awkward, the whole project goes kaput.'

'Then what will you do?' he asked.

'It won't happen—it can't. I won't let him win.'

'Perhaps he's really not as bad as you imagine. Maybe you can talk him into some sort of compromise?'

'Huh! We'll see about that. I'm not going down without a fight, whatever happens!' Pagan declared.

'That's the spirit,' he agreed tonelessly. Then he gave her a quizzical look. 'When I arrived just now I thought I stood a chance of not being given the brush-off today. How do you rate my chances now?'

'Who knows?' She lowered her long lashes and then looked back at him.

'Shall I risk it?' he teased.

'That's up to you.' Her heart pumped furiously.

'All right. What about a meal this evening?'

'Lovely,' she smiled. 'But I'd better warn you, there are only deadly expensive hotels or chicken take-aways.'

'There must be something in between,' he chided.

'Are you staying in a hotel?' she asked.

'If you can call it that,' he laughed deprecatingly. 'But it wouldn't be suitable.' His eyes slid the length of her body and back. When she caught his eye she blushed, but he was smiling. There was a pause.

'Do you have any transport?' he asked.

She nodded. 'It's no good living round here without a car.'

'Then meet me in town somewhere about eight? We'll

decide then where we want to go, after I've asked around.'

Pagan nodded. That sounded fine. It would give her chance to have a shower and slip into something plain. Maybe she'd even wear trousers and a light summer blouse. She didn't want to make the mistake of looking overdressed, and it was unlikely that they would be going anywhere really special. She looked at his cut-down denims and the blue rubber flip-flops. He was wearing a dark blue T-shirt today, and though it was the sort of cheap summer garb hundreds of men wore, on him it seemed to have an indefinable something, perhaps because of the exotic contrast it made with his hair and his deep tan. It was unpretentious gear, though, to say the least.

'Maybe we'll go to a disco afterwards. Do you like dancing?' he asked.

Pagan nodded. To be truthful, she didn't even know. Discos weren't exactly John's scene and she seemed to have missed out on all that sort of thing together with the teenage years. Suddenly she felt as if she had a lot of catching up to do. As if, all at once, something of her lost past could be regained. Maybe she was silly going out with someone who had simply sailed into her life out of the blue, but she couldn't help it. She didn't care that he wasn't well off. He seemed to have such an aura of fun about him, as if he was the sort of person who could make anything happen just by wanting it badly enough.

I'm falling for him, she told herself in sudden wonder. This must be what it is to fall in love. Her eyes were shining.

'Eight o'clock it is, then.'

They fixed a place to meet, and in a sort of dreamy haze Pagan watched him launch the sailboard smoothly on to the water and allow himself to be borne back along the lake.

When she got back to the boathouse the first thing

she did was to ring Faynia. First she apologised for
being unable to make it that evening. Then she asked
that Faynia would convey her apologies to John.

'I just can't tell him that I'm having a date with
somebody else. Not yet. I feel too confused. I feel——'
she paused, searching for the right word, 'I feel sort of
all buzzy. I've never felt like this before. It's peculiar.'

'It's called infatuation, darling. Don't let me spoil
things, but I'd say you're suffering from an advanced
attack. You also seem to be a perfect example of
retarded adolescence. Most girls go through this stage
in their early teens. All I can say is just watch your
step.' Faynia's voice, despite the flippancy of her words,
held a note of concern. 'He's on holiday here, I
suppose? A marauding male looking for a bit of holiday
fun, no less?'

'I know all that,' Pagan gripped the phone tightly,
'I'm not stupid, Faynia. And it was you who scolded
me for turning my nose up at him in the first place.
Anyway, I shan't do anything silly——'

'Only fall head over heels for a complete stranger.'

'He's not a *complete* stranger.'

'No?'

'We've talked. He seems—oh, I feel as if I've known
him all my life.'

'Yes. I used to have that feeling too. When I was
around about your mental age at the moment, which
I'd put generously at about twelve,' commented Faynia
drily. 'Seriously, I think you need a chaperone.'

Pagan protested, 'He's all *right*!'

'He may be a mass murderer on the run from the
police, for all you know.'

'What? Sailing about openly on the lake?' scoffed
Pagan. 'And anyway, he'd need to go about in a black
bag not to be recognised. He's so distinctive-looking, so
devastatingly out of the ordinary. He'd never be able to
disguise himself sufficiently to be on the run from
anywhere.'

'What's the name of this paragon, then?' cut in Faynia, unimpressed.

Pagan paused. She heard a muttered exclamation at the other end of the line. Faynia's voice was scathing when it came. 'You really are a nut case!' she exclaimed. 'The world is full of wolves. They eat little innocents like you for breakfast. I think we'd better arrange to rendezvous somewhere quite by accident this evening. Get him to take you to Renoir's, that's informal enough for anyone. And do,' she added, 'try to find out his name before we meet so that you can introduce us.'

CHAPTER THREE

WHEN Pagan at last drew up in her little Renault in the market place, she was a bundle of nerves.

'What if he doesn't turn up?' she thought, biting her lower lip and scanning the front of the wine bar where they were to meet.

But she needn't have worried. Almost before she had had time to turn the key in the lock, she saw him coming out, and her heart missed half a dozen beats at the sight of him.

He looked devastatingly masculine in close-fitting white levis and a fine dark wool sweater that seemed to mould itself to his torso. Over one shoulder he carried a pale-coloured jacket lined in Burberry plaid, and when his eyes alighted on her his tanned face broke into a smile of welcome.

As he walked with almost calculated slowness towards her Pagan couldn't help drinking in the way he looked.

His fair, sun-streaked hair seemed to shine with health and good grooming and although he was dressed so casually there was an unmistakable air of polished masculinity about him that made her quicken her steps with anticipation.

Although she had told Faynia that she felt she had known him for ages there were a million questions she needed to ask, and a wide smile broke across her face as they drew level.

'I hope I'm not late——' she broke out.

'I came out just in case you felt shy at coming in there by yourself——' he began at the same time.

They both laughed.

'You're not late at all,' he said softly, eying her from head to foot.

'That was nice of you,' she replied to his first remark. 'I've never been to a wine bar alone before.'

They both laughed again. Then he took her by the arm.

His smile had widened. 'I'm not surprised about that,' he said, taking up her last remark. 'You look devastating—as if you never have to go anywhere alone.'

Before she had time to recover from a remark like that he had taken hold of her by both elbows and drew her to him, oblivious to the stares of the passersby.

'I've been doing a little research since we last met and I'm told there's a nice little restaurant down by the lake. Shall we give it a try?'

Pagan nodded, scarcely hearing what he said, her heart thumping violently at the proximity of his hard, muscled body. Briefly she remembered Faynia's concern and their arrangement to meet at Renoir's later on. She would mention it some time. If things started to get out of control.

'Do you mind driving?' he asked, bending his head to her so that she could feel the warmth of his breath brush against her cheek.

Again she shook her head.

Unexpectedly he remarked: 'You look very different this evening. What have you done?'

'Nothing much,' she replied innocently, shutting out with an effort the hours she had spent agonising over what to wear and how to have her hair. Mentally she thanked Faynia for making her buy the jade satin dungarees she now wore.

He looked at her through narrowed eyes for a moment as if surprised by something about her, then abruptly he turned her round and, his arm still around her waist, walked her back towards the car. When they reached it he put his hand over the top of hers as she inserted the key in the lock.

'Wait a moment. Would you rather go by taxi?'

'Taxi? Here? We'd be hard put to it to find one, I'm afraid.'

'That's what I thought,' he shrugged. 'I hate asking you to drive.'

'It doesn't matter,' she answered lightly. 'I suppose you thought you wouldn't need your car on holiday.' She opened the passenger door and asked casually, 'What do you usually drive?'

He was just about to get in when he stopped abruptly as if confused. He gave her a quick assessing look. Then without replying he swung down into the passenger seat. When Pagan got in beside him he was making a great show of hunting around for the seat-belt.

'It's quite straightforward,' she told him drily, pulling the thick belt from its coil under the seat. 'What do you usually drive?' she repeated.

He caught her glance and grimaced.

'The usual sort of thing,' he told her with a crooked smile.

'Oh, I see,' she murmured, giving him a quizzical glance. She felt put out by the sudden reticence in his manner, as if he was holding out on her. Without saying anything, she started the engine and in no time they had left the town behind and were bowling along the lake road in the direction he indicated.

Some time later, after a pleasant enough meal, Pagan leaned back in her chair and regarded him with eyes which expressed the puzzlement she was beginning to feel.

Although she couldn't help noticing that his attention had never strayed from her all evening, she was also powerfully aware of some block between them that made conversation somehow less than easy. Something unspoken seemed to lie between them.

'You're adept at drawing people out,' she told him rather mockingly. 'You've hardly told me anything about yourself, except your name—Leale.'

His eyes gleamed with amusement. He looked insufferably charming, she thought, determined not to let her feelings sway her too much in his favour.

'There's not an awful lot to say about me, really,' he murmured, taking her hand where it lay on the tablecloth. Pagan bit back the impulse to speak and he was forced to go on to fill in the lengthening silence with, 'I'm just an ordinary sort of chap.' He paused again, but again she let him go on.

'I'm thirty-four, mad about windsurfing, like travel, good food, good music.' He avoided her eyes. 'That's about it.'

She withdrew her hand. It was impossible to gauge the meaning in his reluctance to meet her eye. There was another uncomfortable silence.

A cold hand seemed to sweep over her body. If ever a man had said 'Keep Off', surely this was it?

This time the silence lengthened. His reticence now only served to fire her curiosity, and, she hated to admit it, to fan the flames of suspicion.

Why was he being so secretive about himself? What was he trying so painstakingly to conceal from her?

She looked him directly in the eye, but he ignored the offer of a second chance with a small noncommittal shrug. She watched as wordlessly he took out a slim, dark cheroot, and lit it from the candle without once looking at her.

She felt as if she had been slapped in the face. All evening she had been allowed to chatter on, even telling him about her ambition to try for the Transatlantic, and it was as if she had bared her soul to him, only to be met now by a cold rebuff on her very first question. She couldn't have felt worse if she had had a bucket of cold water thrown over her.

Of course, her thoughts raced, it could mean only one

thing. He was almost surely married. The glaring omission in his résumé told her that clearly enough. But then what else had she expected?

She started to get to her feet.

'Where are you going?' He put out a hand and forced her firmly back into her chair.

Her voice was colder than it had been formerly when she told him, 'I said I might call in at Renoir's later this evening.'

She said the name as if it was an old haunt of hers, instead of a place she had merely heard about second-hand from Faynia.

'Renoir's?' he queried.

'Just a club.' Pagan gave a bored shrug. 'There's dancing.'

'So you don't spend every night poring over log books?' He grinned, as if nothing was the matter. 'I thought it was too good to be true!' His eyes slid teasingly over her body and came back to alight on her face.

Pagan flushed with annoyance. Her honesty had never been so deliberately doubted before.

Rather than put him right she glared back at him without answering. Angry with herself for telling him the secret dreams she had shared with no one else, and angry because her life didn't live up to his, it was hard to have the truth suddenly revealed to her—that this special evening was in no way special for him. What had Faynia called their date?—a bit of holiday fun.

She drew herself up. Well, she'd done with revealing all her most private hopes and ambitions. It was pearls before swine. If he wanted to poke and pry into her life from now on he would have to share some of his own secrets with her.

'Well, what are we waiting for?' she demanded almost rudely.

'The bill, that's all.' He regarded her with a sardonic lift of the eyebrows as she started to get to her feet.

'Personally I wouldn't mind coming back here,' he told her, 'so I think I'd prefer to leave after seeing to the usual formalities.'

Pagan blushed with annoyance and sat down again until Leale caught the waiter's eye and settled the bill. She noticed that he used an American Express card, and what was more she let him notice she'd seen it. But she didn't say anything, merely turning her head when she saw he had observed the direction of her glance.

'I travel a lot,' he told her laconically, sitting back in his chair and to her annoyance making no effort to leave now that nothing was keeping them.

'Really?' she asked in as bored a tone as she could muster. She bit back the words on the end of her tongue. Hell, what did it matter what his job was, or whether he was just a bum moving on from town to town, or whether he travelled with his wife, or whoever? Give him his due, she thought bitterly, he hasn't actually tried anything on. He'd admitted he was lonely for company. They were simply having a quiet meal together. Just because he was so gorgeous and looked at her in that lazy, teasing way that sent her body into a glow of desire, here she was building the thing into the beginnings of a passionate affair.

As Faynia had so neatly put it, she was a prime example of retarded adolescence. Anyone else would have seen through his phoney charm at once. It was a good job he wouldn't be around long, at least she wasn't going to have time to get her fingers burnt.

'I thought you wanted to go?' The words cut into her thoughts.

'You're right.' She rose abruptly to her feet.

'Pagan.' He stood up and moved swiftly to her side, taking her by the arm with an air of concern that almost had her convinced. 'Are you angry about something?'

'Not at all,' she replied coolly. 'What on earth have I to be angry about? It was quite a pleasant meal.' Her gaze met his without blinking.

A shadow momentarily crossed his face. Then his grip on her arm relaxed.

'I don't know why you're in such a hurry all of a sudden. But if you want to, we'll go.'

When they were back in the car Leale casually put his hand along the back of her seat. 'Pagan——' he turned to her and she could see the outlines of his face in the dark, illumined only by the coloured lights round the car park. He was looking at her without speaking and she felt a tremor like little charges of electricity flicker up and down her spine.

He's going to kiss me now, she thought. Restively she moved her head. They were so cramped in her little car, it was dangerous sitting in such close proximity to such a man. She could feel the soft wool of his sweater touching her bare neck and imperceptibly she became aware that he was beginning to draw her slowly towards him.

'No!' she blurted, punching at his broad chest with both hands. 'I don't want——' But his hand was gently circling the back of her neck and she felt him drawing her closer to him again. Just when she thought his full sensuous lips were about to come irresistibly down on her own, just when she thought she was going to be well and truly kissed if that was what he wanted, he paused, and she felt him draw back slightly. His eyes searched her face for some sign of response.

'Is that no-no, or no-yes?' he asked quietly.

The irresistible momentum of his slow approach was halted for a moment. She made the most of it to retort, much against her will, 'It's no-no, of course. I don't play games.'

With a mixture of relief and disappointment she felt his grip slacken. 'I'm sorry.'

Could she believe her ears? He was actually apologising! Did such men exist? She looked at him out of the corners of her eyes. He looked quite genuinely sorry. She felt confused. Now she wanted nothing more than to feel the soft power of his lips on hers. Then she remembered his reticence all evening and reluctantly she put the key into the ignition.

'It isn't far to Renoir's,' she told him in a small, choky, matter-of-fact voice.

He didn't reply, and she had to drive the three or four miles back along the lake road without a word being exchanged between them.

When they went down the steps into the basement bar there was no sign of Faynia and the rest of the crowd, and after a drink in which neither of them seemed to be able to find anything to say Leale asked her if she would like to dance.

'I'm feeling rather tired,' she told him mendaciously with an already prepared excuse. 'I think I'd like to go home now.'

Without a word of comment he wrapped her jacket round her shoulders, and they were on the point of coming out into the street when Pagan almost cannoned into someone.

'Pagan! So you did manage to make it after all!' John's pleased expression changed at once as Leale came out of the club behind her and put an arm protectively around her waist.

Pagan felt his grip tighten when he realised the shock-haired boy was addressing her. She looked from one to the other.

'This is a surprise, John. And what bad timing—I've already had enough of this evening and I'm just on my way home.' Thinking quickly, she turned to Leale. 'Thank you for the drink and so on,' she told him coolly. 'See you around some time, perhaps. Goodbye.'

Then with a toss of her head she turned on her heel and, swinging her car keys from their ring, she made her way as nonchalantly as she knew how, across the park to the Renault, leaving both men standing on the pavement.

As she gunned the car, she was in time to see Leale

detach himself from the group outside the club and make as if to come across the park towards her. But she put her foot hard down on the accelerator and was out through the gates and swinging into the main road before he could get near enough to do anything about it.

She had the glum satisfaction of seeing him gazing after her as she sped off down the road.

It was the shrilling of the telephone beside her bed and not the alarm set for seven-thirty that awoke her next morning.

She stretched out a hand and felt around for the handpiece without opening her eyes. It must be horribly early, she thought, with irritation. The voice at the other end was halting in its apologies. It was John, and he was obviously talking quietly so as not to disturb anyone else at the house so early on a Sunday morning.

'I couldn't sleep, Pagan. Are you all right?'

'Of course I'm all right,' she replied, bewildered. 'A bit cross at being woken up *before* my alarm. Is it as early as it seems?' She swivelled to have a look at the clock. Just after seven. What on earth was up? 'What on earth are you playing at, John? Do you realise what the time is?'

'I'm sorry, I wanted to catch you before you went out.'

'Nine o'clock might have done it, don't you think?'

'I couldn't sleep.'

'*You* can't sleep, no one sleeps, is that it? Oh well—' she yawned, 'what do you want?'

Slowly the memory of the previous night's brief encounter was seeping back into her sleep-befuddled brain. Had she been rotten to him? Yes, she had. She was about to say she was sorry when she realised he was doing some apologising himself. She listened as he went on.

'It was because she told me you wouldn't be coming

out at all if you hadn't made it by nine-thirty. And we all waited and when you didn't turn up we decided to go somewhere Faynia knew about. It wasn't all that marvellous, rather noisy actually, and I wanted to come back to Renoir's. Well, really, Pagan, to be honest, it was to see if you'd changed your mind, but Faynia insisted on coming back too, and she'd just sort of put her arm sort of in mine as we got to the door and then you came charging out. It wasn't what it seemed, honestly. It was more of a friendly gesture than anything else——'

'What?' Pagan tried to focus on what he was telling her.

'I'm saying we only came back to see if you were there.'

Pagan sat up. 'It wasn't likely I'd still be there at midnight, waiting, was it?' she asked reasonably.

John sounded nettled. 'But you were there,' he replied promptly. 'I feel bad at the thought that you were waiting for me all that time. I can understand why you feel mad at me. I'd just assumed you wouldn't still be waiting at that time of night——'

'Hold on a minute! I thought you just said you thought I *would* be there.' Pagan smiled grimly. She didn't know what all this was about, but she didn't mind obligingly pointing out the inconsistencies in John's masculine logic. She sighed while he tried to disentangle himself from the knot he'd tied himself up in. All she wanted, now she was awake, was a nice hot cup of black coffee.

She scrambled up on to her knees to have a look at the lake, the phone still chattering on, resting on her shoulder.

Lovely—it was another good day for the beginners. Just enough of a breeze, by the look of the treetops, to make it interesting, but not enough to scare them.

She snuggled back under the duvet and when a pause came up, she said into the phone, 'John, may I say something?' She waited for his cautious 'Yes'. It didn't seem fair to let him labour under the apparent delusion that her abrupt greeting and sudden departure the night before had had anything to do with the fact that Faynia had been clinging to his arm. Heavens, she hadn't even *noticed* Faynia. She had been too concerned by the fact that her evening with Leale had somehow been spoiled and that, instead of its being the beginning of something, they were on the point of ending whatever little there had been.

She chose her words carefully. 'I'm not angry about anything, John. Things just didn't work out. It doesn't matter. No hard feelings.'

'Don't say that, please, darling,' he pleaded. 'Things *will* work out for us, if you give me just one more chance. It was a silly mistake, that's all. You mean such a lot to me. I realise I've been very casual towards you, but don't let's end it just because of a stupid misunderstanding.'

Pagan couldn't say anything for a moment. John was really taking things seriously this morning. Now he thought she didn't want to see him at all, that she was jealous, angry and hurt about the previous night's trivial incident. How could she explain, and have him believe her, that she really hadn't given him more than a passing thought last night? He was a nice enough boy, and she didn't want to lose his friendship over something so silly.

'I'm still a bit sleepy,' she told him. 'My head's all woolly and I can't think straight.'

'Don't make any decision yet, darling. Let me come and see you, and we'll talk things over calmly and rationally.'

'Fine, fine,' agreed Pagan absently. She couldn't inject much enthusiasm into her voice, for the full memory of the previous night had come back, and all she could see was the receding figure of a muscular blond man in white levis framed in her rear-view

mirror. Then the image was gone, swallowed up by the
night.

John was saying something about seeing her later
that day. She told him she was working all day. He told
her to expect him when she finished. Pagan hadn't the
energy to put him off. What did it matter? He was all
right. She didn't object to his putting his arm round
Faynia or even Faynia putting her arm in his. It was all
one to her what they both did.

She replaced the receiver with a little sigh.

Of the red, white and blue sail nothing had been seen all
morning. Its absence perversely enough made Pagan
feel quite irritable.

Lunchtime came around and she was just about to
join the rest of the staff in a pub lunch across the road
when she heard someone call her name, and looking up,
she saw a figure hurrying towards her through the trees
on the edge of the Manor's unkempt garden.

'Pagan, I'm so glad I caught up with you before you
left!'

Her spirits plunged. It was only John. His hair
rumpled as usual, and his boyish face full of concern, he
hurried across the gravel towards her.

When he drew level he said in everyone's hearing,
'You're not mad at me, are you?'

Pagan felt her heart sink with embarrassment. The
last thing she wanted was an emotional scene in full
view of everyone.

'Should I be?' she asked with a little smile, hoping to
laugh it off. 'Don't tell me you've lost that library book
I lent you?'

John looked puzzled and Pagan waited until everyone
was out of earshot before she turned to him and said,
'John, really, I'm busy during the day, you know that.
I'm also very hungry and I want to have some lunch
now.'

'That's all right,' he told her. 'Have lunch on me.' He

took her possessively by the arm and before she could disentangle herself, he was leading her off down the lane.

She had never seen him behaving so masterfully, and it was only when he turned to her that she caught the whiff of alcohol on his breath.

'John, I don't want any scenes in front of everyone. It wouldn't look good.'

He tightened his hold on her. 'I'm not going to cause any scenes. It's that I desperately wanted to see you.' He regarded her cautiously as if trying to guess her mood. 'You looked so fantastic last night,' he told her in a low voice. 'I've never seen you look like that before. It made me realise how——' he hesitated, 'how I wanted you.'

He pulled her to a stop by the edge of the shrubbery. 'I've been doing some thinking and at the time what Faynia told me didn't seem to ring true—about you not being sure whether you'd be at Renoir's last night. It's not like you to suddenly change your mind about a date. Then when I saw you with that man it made me wonder.'

'What did it make you wonder?' she asked, curious despite herself.

'Well, whether you're as—demure as you seem to make out.' He paused, and the hesitation on his face told her that he was thinking he might have already gone too far, but he seemed to make a visible effort and went on: 'They tell me no girl likes a man to give her the kid glove treatment. And I suppose I've always taken your "no" to mean just that.'

His grip tightened and as she tried to move away he pressed her body closer to his own. Again she smelt the slight whiff of alcohol on his breath.

'That's not just communion sherry, is it?' she accused, stepping back. But he was too quick and managed to keep his arms wrapped round her, pulling her close again.

He ignored her imputation and said instead, 'I don't mind admitting I felt jealous when I saw you with someone else. I'd always thought I could trust you.'

'Trust me? What do you mean by that? Trust me to sit at home every night? Now why should you imagine I'd do a thing like that?'. Pagan was annoyed now. Here she was having her movements questioned by this—this *boy*!

'We owe each other nothing,' she told him, looking him levelly in the eye. 'I don't question you about other girl-friends and I don't expect you to question me. As for being jealous, that's rather an extreme reaction, isn't it?'

'No, Pagan, no,' he told her earnestly. 'That's what I'm trying to say. Everything's changed. From the moment I saw you standing there in those satin dungarees with your hair in that sexy style and your make-up and everything so glamorous-looking about you I knew I'd been handling the whole thing the wrong way.'

He pulled her face towards his and tried to plant a kiss on her lips. She turned her head, but he thought she was teasing and increased the pressure on the back of her neck.

'Ow!' she cried, trying to push him away, but he brought his lips down hard and she felt his usually boyish kiss become harshly demanding, quite unlike the goodnight peck on the cheek she was used to. Anger rose up quickly making her bite him hard on the lip. With a swift jerk of her body she freed herself and stood panting an arm's length away.

'Gosh, you're so exciting, Pagan!' John told her, not at all angry. 'I never realised before just how—how——' he paused.

'How much of a mind of her own the lady has,' broke in a sardonic voice from behind them, and Pagan turned to see the hawklike bronzed face of Leale split into a grin of derision as he pushed his way through the shrubbery.

'Trespassing again,' said Pagan cuttingly, before he could say another word. She felt utterly mortified. That he should have seen her in John's arms! Not that it made much difference. He could see her in the arms of a hundred men, and it wouldn't make any difference to the fact that he was only interested in the power of his own phoney charm on her.

John looked angrily at Leale as he stepped arrogantly between them.

'Now perhaps we can have a replay of that little scene last night. Although this time you'd better stay,' he told Pagan curtly.

She opened her mouth, but closed it again. Leale had turned his back on her and was looking down at John. The younger man didn't say anything, and neither did Leale. Nothing much seemed to happen for a minute or two, but suddenly John seemed to be walking off rather quickly down the lane and Leale was turning back towards Pagan, a cold smile on his face. He took hold of her by the waist and dragged her to him.

'You ran out on me,' he said through scarcely parted lips. 'No one, but no one has ever run out on me before.'

'There's a first time for everything,' croaked Pagan, trying to pull away from him. His presence did such strange things to her body she could scarcely trust herself to stand up.

His arms were circling her gently. 'I don't usually go eavesdropping in shrubberies,' he told her, 'but I couldn't help overhearing what that young puppy was saying to you.'

'You had no right to make him go away like that,' she admonished weakly.

'Oh dear, did I upset him, do you think? But I didn't say a word!' He tried to look apologetic, without success.

'You've no need to *say* anything.' Even though she knew he was putting her on, she felt herself sinking into the circle of his arms, and all her anger drained away. 'You're a big bully,' she began to protest. 'You seem to think 'one look from you is enough!'

She let him bring his face close to hers. 'Isn't it?' he mocked, searching her flushed face, with an air of what seemed like satisfaction. 'The first thing he's got to learn about you is when you say no you mean it. Isn't that right?' His lips scarcely moved when he spoke.

She felt him draw her closer still so that the length of his body exactly matched her own. He tilted her head back; as her eyes closed his lips searched for her own, and then for a long time there was nothing at all but the ecstasy of his touch.

Breathlessly they parted, only to come together again in a swooning delight of pure pleasure.

Then he held her at arm's length. 'It isn't only lunch you're hungry for!' he mocked.

His frankness made her blush.

'Come on, I'll buy you a decent lunch at the pub to set you up for this afternoon. You're a hard-working little lady,' he told her with something like approval in his eyes, as he began to walk her up the lane to the main road. 'But all sailors need food.'

Her mind swimming in confusion, Pagan allowed him to lead her to the top of the lane. Then she pulled back. What was she doing allowing this self-confident, triumphantly smiling Adonis to lead her about as if she was his latest conquest? Her reputation would be shot to pieces if she allowed him to march her into the bar in front of everybody with his arm proprietorially over her shoulders! There was only one conclusion they would come to after one look at him.

'Do you mind?' she asked, disengaging her arm from his. 'I have to work with these people.

The slight frown that showed itself on his face told her that he was unused to women putting up a resistance to him. But instead of crossing the road to the bar of the Three Jolly Anglers he drew her on in the direction of the pub further down the road.

'Pity I haven't got a car with me,' he said, with a strange little smile. 'We could find some nice out-of-the-way little place where we could be as indiscreet as we pleased.'

They were passing the front of the Manor now, and Pagan couldn't help noticing the car parked on the drive in front of it. It was colossal, some foreign make she didn't recognise, and it looked very, very fast. Evidently the new owner had turned up at last.

Leale had just tucked her hand in his and, turning towards her with that lazy smile calculated to charm the birds off the trees, said, 'I guess it's confession time right now——' when a low-slung sports car spurting gravel from beneath white-walled tyres came to a sudden grinding halt beside them.

Pagan had scarcely had time to react to the tremor of fear his words provoked. Oblivious to the hooting of car horns as the traffic began to pile up behind her, the driver's window was wound down and a high, girlish voice called out, 'Leale! So there you are! We've been sending out search parties for you. There's an urgent message from Carter—he's nearly climbing up the wall with rage!'

Pagan felt Leale stiffen. His hand, which had been holding hers, dropped to his side.

The girl smiled up at him, then, opening the door of the sports car, she swung her long shapely legs, clad in sheer black nylons and high-heeled spiky sandals, to the ground.

Leale's glance seemed to sweep over her and come back to rest on the legs.

Why not? thought Pagan with a sudden painful feeling like a knife stabbing at her heart. They were gorgeous and so, regrettably, was the rest of her. She was tall and vividly blonde, and her laughing eyes came level with Leale's shoulder. Slowly she raised her large dark-fringed eyes to him and gave him an innocent look. 'Leale,' she said huskily, 'you're wicked!' She gave another girlish laugh and put her hand on his arm. 'I've had the devil's own job to keep Carter from jumping on the first flight back to town. He needs your signature. I persuaded him to wait for you back at the hotel. He'll still be there, clutching his little papers to his chest. But I really think you should have let us know where you'd be—everyone was worried.'

She gave a quickly appraising look at Pagan. 'I told him you were probably on the job,' she gave a snigger, 'and not to worry. But you know what an old maid he is. He was worried that you'd be gone for the rest of the day. I said, I doubt that, there's nothing to distract him to that extent around here.'

She gave a trilling laugh and let her eyes wander back to the hunched figure of Pagan standing a few yards away where Leale had left her. Turning back, she gave him an up-and-down smile and her hand seemed to tighten possessively on his arm. 'I have a feeling he wants to take you back with him.'

'Let's go, then.' Leale was all action. He was round at the passenger door in two strides and asking, 'Did he say what was so important?'

The girl shook her head before folding herself elegantly back into the driver's seat. She gave a brief quizzical glance in Pagan's direction before starting the engine.

She wasn't as old as Pagan had taken her to be in that first split-second of sight when she had first alighted from the car. But she was extremely sophisticated in a sharp, polished sort of way, in a multi-coloured two-piece, her hair coiled in a sleek knot on top of her head. She made Pagan, clad in jeans and sweater, feel suddenly gauche and adolescent.

Just as he was about to swing down into the

passenger seat, Leale stopped as if he had suddenly remembered something. He glanced across the top of the car towards Pagan and said: 'This looks like another small emergency.' He shrugged.

Miserably Pagan stared back at him. The girl was evidently keen to get away, because any words she might have uttered would have been drowned in the sound of the engine as the blonde gunned it, impatient to be off.

But before she could slide away Leale said, 'Hold it a minute,' and began to stride back towards Pagan.

'I don't know what's blown up. I'll be in touch—don't worry. We'll have to have a talk.' He bent to brush her lightly on the forehead with his lips. Then, before she could do more than stand and stare, he was climbing into the car beside the girl and then the car was disappearing rapidly up the road in a spray of gravel and loose mud.

Pagan stared after them both in disbelief. So that was that, was it?

In a confusion of feelings she paced disconsolately across towards the Three Jolly Anglers.

So he'd be in touch, would he? Wonderful! How long would she have to wait? Half an hour? A day? A week? And what was she supposed to do in the meantime—sit and dream of him?

And who was that woman? Was she his wife? His mistress? Her sophisticated gloss was anything but wifely. And what was she doing here? Wasn't he supposed to be on holiday? Did that mean they were holidaying together? Why, then, was she chasing him up to sign papers? And why, too, was he always slipping away from her to come out to the landing?

Pagan kicked a stone along in front of her as she walked along.

He had promised a confession. She shivered. As far as I'm concerned, it can wait for ever, she told herself angrily. She wasn't a toy, to be picked up and put down at random like this. She was a human being with a life of her own.

Damn him, she thought as she slammed into the bar, who did he think he was, sailing into her life and turning its uneventful tranquillity into such confusion?

CHAPTER FOUR

IT was lateish the next morning when a stream of sunlight through the big french windows woke her up.

There was a little nub of rancour somewhere in the back of her mind, but for a moment she couldn't recall why it was there and she lay, warm and content, in the sunlight for a moment or two. Then with an exclamation she was throwing back the duvet and springing out of bed.

No time for going over yesterday's woes. She had to get up, don the new Liberty print suit Faynia had lent her, and exert her charm on this man de Laszlo.

She showered briskly, then came back into the bedroom to dress. Faynia would probably scold her if she didn't do the suit justice, and she dabbed a little gloss on her lips and cheeks and drew a swift smear of liner under her eyes as a small concession to her. That would have to do.

Besides, she excused herself, this de Laszlo was a money-man, judging by the car he drove. He wouldn't be interested in whether she wore make-up or woad. All she had to do was to convince him she meant business.

With an unwonted flicker of apprehension, she ran over the facts in her head. Really she knew she was finally dependent on his goodwill. Everything would hang on what type of man he was, mean or charitable, flexible or a stickler after his own rights. It was a favour she was going to ask, and though she had made sure she was in a position to pay for whatever rights he granted her, there was still the big stumbling block of whether he would feel inclined to do what she was going to ask.

It was just on ten-thirty when she swung her old Renault round the last bend in the long, tree-lined drive which led down, past a paddock full of aristocratic-looking horses, to the forecourt of the hotel where de Laszlo was waiting. Waiting, she thought fatalistically, with her destiny in his hands.

She walked briskly up the wide steps into the vestibule and looked round for reception. On the far side of what seemed like miles of echo-deadening carpet was a tiny gilt and mahogany desk at which sat an immaculate brunette. She gave Pagan a professional smile and asked her to wait. Uneasily Pagan perched herself on the edge of a little gilt chair and tried not to gaze around with her mouth open.

'*Very* exclusive,' Faynia had pronounced through half-closed eyes. And Pagan quite saw what she meant.

It was more like an elegant country house than a commercial enterprise, and she was almost surprised that well-dressed children accompanied by an aproned nanny were not at play on the smooth turf beyond the terrace.

Lost in reverie, she scarcely heard the arrival of the man across the deep pile carpet until the subdued tones of his voice brought her back with a sudden rush. He was about fifty, balding, dressed unexceptionally in a dark business suit. He carried a black leather portfolio under his arm, and with his other hand he was indicating that she should follow him to the lift.

In a few moments she was being ushered into what seemed to be a temporary office, and she found herself sinking down on to a brown velvet sofa as de Laszlo went behind the desk which stood over by the window to take out some papers from the black leather portfolio. As he riffled through them she noted that he had quite an unexpectedly pleasant face, almost cherubic, and this impression was confirmed when he lifted his eyes and gave her a twinkling smile.

'I apologise for the delay, my dear. Mr de Laszlo won't be long now.'

Pagan's eyes widened.

As if in answer to the question there he reached across the desk saying: 'Brangwyn's the name—I'm one of Mr de Laszlo's accountants.'

The rest of his words were drowned out by the sound of what Pagan took to be the mountain rescue helicopter flying very low overhead. A shadow crossed the window and the noise rose to a deafening pitch for a moment, then slackened and finally died.

Mr Brangwyn was standing at the window looking on to the lawn. He gave a smile of satisfaction before turning back into the room.

'He won't be too long now,' he told her, and Pagan was doubtful as to how he could be so sure merely by looking through a window which was on the opposite side of the building to the car park.

The buzzer sounded again, cutting through her thoughts, and Mr Brangwyn looked at her. 'Here he is now.' In that phrase there was no warning of the shock that was to follow.

There came a few seconds pause then the door was flung open and at last in came de Lazlo himself. His presence seemed to fill the room. Tall, blond and broad-shouldered, he was all vibrant masculinity.

Pagan gawked at the hawklike planes and contours of his bronzed face, which were now schooled into an expression of masculine toughness. An expensive topcoat was draped casually over his shoulders, its dark cloth contrasting with the pale worsted of his Savile Row suit. That he ever adorned that muscular body, its tough virility ill-concealed in its expensive apparel, in anything like a pair of bleached, cut-down denim shorts and a simple black T-shirt, there was now no evidence. He looked every inch the successful businessman, polished, groomed, and superbly turned out, and as hard and expensive-looking as cut diamonds.

Pagan was unaware that she had risen to her feet. She felt as if she was drowning in the sheer leonine power of his appearance. A shudder of something like fear shook through her body, even before he walked towards her, his eyes jetting silver sparks of amusement at her evident confusion.

'You?' she grated when she at last found her voice. Her heart lurched and she fought for control. Total confusion seemed to paralyse her for a moment, but before she could utter a word, Leale had turned to Mr Brangwyn and with a nod, dismissed him.

Pagan leashed in her feelings until she heard the door click discreetly behind him. Then, coiled for the attack, she swung on him.

'So?' she spat. 'What sort of a game are you playing—Mr de Laszlo!'

Leale laughed easily. 'I thought there were going to be squalls when I saw your expression,' he told her with an infuriating smile as he advanced towards her.

'Don't you put your hands on me!' she cried, backing away from his approach until she was almost touching the wall. 'I don't know what satisfaction you get out of all this trickery, but you've made one very big mistake!'

Leale laughed again, softly, so that Pagan felt that if she had been a cat she would have spread her claws and drawn them in a scarlet trace down the side of his tanned and insufferably handsome face.

'Squalls was an understatement. It's going to be storm force ten all the way,' he observed.

Ignoring his deep chuckle of amusement, she demanded, 'Well? Would you care to explain yourself?' Her voice was hoarse with fury.

Leale prudently kept himself an arm's length away. 'I can't see why you're so angry. You made such a lot of assumptions about the new owner of the Manor—and, I suspect, about me, on that first meeting—that it seemed difficult not to let it go on. I thought if I'd announced that *I* was the fascist you were in such a stew about on Saturday you wouldn't have had that meal with me that night. Somehow or other, between our little games, there never seemed to be an appropriate moment to tell you the truth. Then, yesterday, when I finally made up my mind to come clean, I was suddenly called away to London on urgent business.'

'London? Ha!' Pagan threw her head back scornfully. 'A likely story, I must say! You seem to be just brim full of lies and subterfuge. Do you honestly expect me to believe a cock-and-bull story like that? I would have thought you might have credited me with a little common sense. How did you go and get back so quickly—by helicopter?'

Leale shrugged deprecatingly, and Pagan, remembering the roar of the engine overhead no more than ten minutes ago, stiffened. Could his story be above-board? But the recollection of how she had been duped blurred her reason. Somehow, to know that he was telling the truth about the London trip made matters worse.

She turned on him in a renewed fury.

'You've really been enjoying yourself, haven't you?' she demanded vehemently. 'What sort of man would behave like this, leading me on to believe that you were just a sailing-bum on a short holiday?'

Her eyes flashed daggers.

'What sort of man—what sort of twisted mind— could think up a trick like that?'

It was the jumbled memory of his kisses and the sudden, ill-timed arrival of the woman in the sports car which fed her rage. With a pang of discomfort she wondered if she too had been a party to the deception.

'If this is the way you get your kicks, I feel sorry for you!' she cried in derision. 'Passing yourself off as someone else! Now I suppose you're going to keep me dangling in suspense just as you did all weekend, holding out the carrot on the stick so that we don't know whether the school can go on or not. That's just the sort of trip to give somebody like you a kick. Mr Power-mad, that's you! I hope you've had your fun, because from now on it's war, and——'

Pagan didn't know what she was going to threaten him with, for at that moment the door opened and the girl from the sports car stood there, a smile of amusement on her face.

'Dear me,' she drawled in wide-eyed innocence. 'Is something the matter, darling?'

Her words could not have been more ill-timed. Without giving Leale chance to utter a word of remonstrance, Pagan picked up her bag and strode towards the door.

As she seemed almost about to push the other woman physically to one side to get through, Leale found his voice and said, quite calmly, 'It's all right—there's no problem with access to the lake. The barbed wire incident was just a misunderstanding by the contractors.'

Pagan turned in the doorway and gave a brittle laugh, her eyes brilliant with anger.

'Do you really expect me to accept that? I'd rather go out of business than depend on charity from *you*! As far as I'm concerned you can boil in hell!'

And she slammed the door behind her—but not without the sound of the other girl's mocking laughter ringing in her ears.

It was a sound that filled her with impotent rage whenever she thought of it.

They were sitting in the back room again, Faynia and she, and there was an open bottle of a rather pleasant wine, some pâté, a little Brie, olives and French bread on a dish beside them, and from the shop as usual floated the strains of the latest hit.

It was raining and Faynia was unperturbed that trade was slack. She had innocently reinstated herself in her former place in Pagan's circle by ringing her up the previous evening, the day of the access debacle as Pagan phrased it, and asking to meet her for a heart to heart at the shop.

After a miserable lunch with Tim and Jan the previous day, when Pagan had briefly sketched in the details of her meeting with Leale de Lazlo—cautiously omitting the latter part of the conversation when she had declined his offer until she had had more time to think it over—she had gratefully told Faynia that she would call in roundabout one.

It was now one-forty-five, and Faynia was gazing at her in perplexity. Offering Pagan the olives, which were declined, she popped one of them into her own mouth and ate on it meditatively.

Still angry, Pagan had told her all that had happened from the moment she had first met Leale in his guise as a sailing bum until the final moment when she had slammed her way out of his office. She described how he had practically egged her on to tell him exactly what she thought of her new neighbour at the Manor.

And Faynia's eyes had darkened. 'The swine!' she interjected. 'That's really hitting below the belt! He deserves all he gets. But, Pagan,' she added curiously, 'whatever made you let him get under your skin like this? He's gorgeous, of course, but you must have had some sign right from the start as to what sort of man he was?'

Pagan's face lost its anger for a moment and became vulnerable.

'Oh, Faynia, I don't know. I just thought I could handle it.' She paused. 'He's far more experienced than me, and so damned cool. I'm just no match for him.' She frowned. 'It was just that there was something about him—his smile. He seemed so open, so warm. It was only on that dreadful Saturday night, when he clammed up whenever I asked him anything personal, that I realised something was wrong.'

'You should have got out then before you really put your foot in it,' said Faynia sagely.

'But I tried, didn't I? I did try. But he pursued me. It was as if he was determined to hunt me down, to trap me into saying all those stupid things.'

'But why would he do a thing like that?' Faynia wrinkled her brow.

'Because he's a cold, sadistic pig and he was determined to make me look like a fool. He's enjoyed stringing me along all weekend. I suppose he expected me to grovel with apologies when he revealed his true identity, and now I'm supposed to fall over myself because he's so graciously deigned to grant me the use of his precious lane. Well, I won't!' Pagan declared fiercely. 'I won't grovel! I hate him!'

'But you know you don't,' butted in Faynia in matter-of-fact tones, 'so you'll just have to tell him you're sorry and thank you very much. Of course,' she added wickedly, 'he's probably changed his mind about you now. After all that, he's probably nailing up the barbed wire himself. Did you really tell him he could boil in hell?'

'That's nothing to what I felt like telling him,' muttered Pagan darkly. 'If that woman hadn't come in I would have.'

'Ah . . .!' said Faynia enigmatically.

'And what's that supposed to mean?'

'That woman?' Faynia raised her delicately arched eyebrows.

'His girl-friend or secretary, I don't know what she is. ... She's a tart—practically crawling all over him, with her silly baby voice!'

'Watch yourself, Pagan,' admonished Faynia. 'Are you talking about a business wrangle or an affair of the heart?'

'Heart? You must be mad! It's that I don't like being made an utter fool of at any time, and certainly not in front of some stupid girl who can do nothing better than claw at his arms with her horrible scarlet nails and simper "Is anything the matter, darling?" in that stupid voice. It makes me see red! All I can say is, they deserve each other. What I want now is to put as much distance between me and them as possible, and if it means moving the school lock, stock and barrel, I will!'

Faynia murmured something soothing and refilled Pagan's wine glass.

'I recommend the Brie,' she said, cutting off two slices. 'Here, try it.'

Without tasting it Pagan popped a piece in her mouth.

'Now,' said Faynia briskly, 'let's forget Mr de Laszlo for a moment, we'll solve that little problem later. Let's turn to matters nearer home. I asked you here because I've something to say to you.' She seemed to take a deep breath. 'John visited me on Sunday, at about the time you were playing castaways with that blond brute, and he was not the John I've grown accustomed to. He was *distraught*, poor love, and looking quite dishevelled—and, Pagan, he seems to have filled a curious little blank in your weekend saga.'

Pagan looked at her dully. John? It seemed aeons ago since she'd given him more than a passing thought.

'If it's about Saturday night,' she brought herself to say, 'then it's quite all right by me if you want to put your arm in his or whatever he was having his guilt feelings about. . . .'

'That's very generous, but it wasn't what was worrying him—at least, not entirely. Apparently you had a somewhat ill-fated little encounter in the lane on Sunday, and he's utterly devastated that the love of a lifetime has been smashed underfoot, first by his own apparent lack of dynamism, which he thinks may have given you only a lukewarm impression of his capabilities, and secondly, by the brutality of your Mr de Laszlo. Tell me,' Faynia leaned forward with interest, 'did they actually come to blows?'

'No,' replied Pagan irritably, not caring whether she disappointed Faynia or not. 'Nothing of the sort. Leale simply looked at him.'

'Looked?'

'You know the way men are. He just looked. And then John walked away.'

'Is that all?'

'I'm sorry it wasn't more exciting.'

Faynia shrugged. 'No doubt you did your best' she paused. 'Men never cease to astonish me. They're all so instinctual, aren't they?'

Faynia smiled complacently. 'If only they had the subtlety and logic of women, that *and* their instinctive brute strength, they'd be invincible!'

'Aren't they?' grimaced Pagan morosely. 'Leale de Laszlo seems to be winning hands down at the moment!'

'That's only because you've let him get under your skin. You've allowed his undoubted physical attractions to make you lose sight of your aims. It seems to me you've got everything going for you at the moment. You've got John on the verge of either suicide or a marriage proposal, and you've got the agreement of de Laszlo to exactly what you wanted——'

'Except that I don't want John, dead or alive, and I can't accept Leale's offer.'

'Silly pride,' returned Faynia. 'It's not going to hurt you to say sorry. And as for John—do you really mean that?'

'Oh, how do I know?' Pagan was exasperated. 'I just don't know. I like him well enough. But how do I know anything?'

'Well,' said Faynia, 'I rather wish you'd make up your mind. For my sake as much as for his.'

'What do you mean?' Pagan's mouth opened.

Faynia grinned sheepishly. 'Perhaps it's my maternal instinct coming out, or perhaps it's something else. It's just that he looked so sweet last night——'

'You saw him last night as well?'

'He practically forced his way into the house, then sat and rambled on about you for hours.' Faynia leaned back in her chair and stretched. 'He's got very nice eyes. I've never noticed that before.'

'His family's loaded too,' rejoined Pagan cynically.

Faynia shrugged. 'That helps of course. But I wouldn't move in on him if I thought you were still involved. Sisterhood and all that.'

Pagan took a deep breath. 'If you want him, you have him. I'm giving up men—they're either fools or pigs. I'm going to dedicate myself to work from now on.' She stood up. 'You're right, Faynia. I've let him make me lose sight of my aims. It won't happen again. From now on I'm going to be as cool as any man and I'm going to use a bit of that subtlety we're supposed to have. No man, but no man, gets the better of me!'

'Your first task must be to tell John your decision', said Faynia. 'To let him off the hook.'

'So he's free to take some other bait?'

Faynia laughed delightedly and without shame. 'Meet him tonight at Renoir's. I'll be there too—to pick up the pieces!'

Pagan left the boutique with a lighter heart, for, whatever her faults, Faynia seemed to have the knack of putting things into a more manageable perspective. If to outsiders she sometimes seemed to be something of a cynical little gold-digger her schemes were never malicious, and she never tried to conceal that what she was after was a husband with a pocket deep enough to satisfy all her material needs. She wasn't averse to hard work herself either, and her little business was evidence of this, so that she herself, beautiful, talented and sophisticated, had a lot to offer in return.

None of this, however, solved the problem of Leale de Laszlo.

The thought of going to him, grovelling at his feet, to say she was sorry, stuck in Pagan's mind, but she could see no way of getting round it. Besides, what if Faynia was right and on the evidence of her behaviour he had decided that she was unsuitable to run a business on what was legally his land?

She could imagine the sadistic pleasure on his face if and when she managed to pluck up enough courage to go to him and beg his forgiveness, when he told her he had changed his mind. She pictured the whole scene in vivid colours, complete with the female companion of the scarlet lips and nails, and she shuddered. It might be cowardice, but there was no way she was going to lay herself open to undergo a scene like that.

Leale's cool blond toughness when she had met him in the office told her clearly enough that he could annihilate her if he so chose. She might be able to put herself together again afterwards, but an audience for such a showdown was not a prospect she relished.

A letter would be the easiest way out. She could let everything be conducted coolly and efficiently by her solicitor—at least, she could do, if that solicitor wasn't, if Faynia was to be believed, rather in love with her. To enlist his aid was somehow just not on.

Pagan had told Faynia she was going to dedicate herself to work from now on, and she was as good as her word. She set off straight back home and settled down at her desk for some serious letter-writing.

A couple of potential sponsors had shown some interest, and she wrote back outlining in more detail her requirements for the Yacht Race, signing off in such a way that it was open for them to fix a meeting in the near future if they were still interested.

The next few days were taken up with the paper-work associated with running the school. There were adverts to place in the sailing magazines, bookings to jigsaw into place, accommodation to fix, and a hundred and one other things to be seen to.

On top of all that, Tim turned up pale-faced for work one morning minus Jan. He had bad news. Jan had collapsed the previous evening at home and the doctor had advised total rest for a few days.

Pagan paid a visit to Jan each morning, but when Pagan suggested getting a replacement for the next weekend course, wan-faced though she was, Jan was adamant that she was going to be back on her feet well before then. Tim was teaching at the nearby comprehensive each day, and Pagan got into the habit of taking some lunch in to share with her. It was on the third day that Jan evidently decided to broach the question of the right of way.

Pagan had been dreading this, because it seemed that no matter how she explained things there was no way in which she could come out of it in a good light. She knew she had been wrong-footed by Leale de Laszlo from the first and she knew that, sympathetic though Jan and Tim would be, it would sow the seeds of a suspicion that she was a risky sort of employer for whom to give up the steady salary from teaching on which the couple at present relied.

Yet she needed Tim and to a lesser extent Jan. It was not only reassuring to feel that there was someone to whom she could talk out the details of future planning for the school's development, it was also essential to have someone reliable who could be trusted to run things properly while she was away.

The Transatlantic was no idle dream. Her brush with Leale de Laszlo had shaken her self-esteem and made her more determined to prove, if only to herself, that she'd got what it takes. Call it pride, egotism, she knew it was more than that. It was also something to do with her uncle, a way of keeping faith with him, repaying him perhaps for looking after her all those years, for confirming the faith in her he evidenced by leaving the school to her.

Quite simply, it was something she had to do.

But the challenge would be that much more difficult to meet if she couldn't rely on the fact that everything at home was running smoothly.

She told Jan again, not altogether untruthfully, that Leale de Laszlo had said there was no problem with their right of way.

'It's simply a question of carrying on as we are,' she hedged. 'I expect eventually we'll have it all nicely tied up in legal jargon.'

Jan gave her a shrewd look. 'You don't seem too happy about it, Pagan. Are there problems we should know about?'

Pagan coloured guiltily and turned her head. 'It's just that de Laszlo is a tricky customer,' she said, picking up some crumbs from the tablecloth and throwing them out of the open doors on to Tim's lovingly paved patio with its stone chimneypots of bright flowers. She lifted her green eyes with an embarrassed frown. 'I suppose you must have heard something about him by now?' she asked.

Jan shook her head. 'News filters through, but I'm feeling pretty much out of things, being confined here for the time being. What's he like?'

'You met him,' replied Pagan, smiling at the bombshell she was about to drop despite herself.

'*I* have? When? Where?'

'He was the chap who took over from you on Sunday afternoon.'

Jan's mouth dropped. 'Did you know it was Leale de Laszlo at the time? I seem to remember you were quite offhand with him.' Her glance at Pagan's expression told her all she needed to know. 'Well,' she exploded, 'what a devil of a trick to pull! I bet you were cross when you found out!'

'Cross isn't in it,' retorted Pagan with a flicker of the old anger.

'Still,' went on Jan cheerfully, 'at least he's said yes, so no harm done. He must be one of those modest millionaires we're always reading about.'

'What?' Pagan's exclamation might have come from the opinion that Leale was a millionaire, something which she might have guessed but hadn't till that moment allowed to cross her mind, but it was in reality due to Jan's ascription of modesty to such a man.

'You must be joking!' she told her. 'There isn't a particle of modesty or humility in him. He's the most arrogant, conceited person I've ever had the misfortune to meet!'

'Oh dear,' murmured Jan, giving her a sidelong look. 'It doesn't augur well to get on the wrong side of one's neighbours.'

'Fortunately,' Pagan retorted to that, 'I'm told, by *one* of his accountants, I'll have you know, that he never stays in one place for very long. So I doubt that we'll be seeing Mr Property-tycoon Laszlo very often at all.'

She left shortly after this.

Earlier, the personal secretary of the promotions manager of one of the firms she had been canvassing had rung to make an appointment. Pagan was gratified that they had been so quick off the mark.

John hadn't taken her seriously when she had talked about her renewed dedication to her career, and now Jan, at lunch-time, had given a small secret smile when she had said much the same thing to her. It was infuriating! But tomorrow she would convince the promotions manager to sponsor her race attempt, and that was all that mattered.

The phone was ringing as she got in and she had to dash to answer it. It was a woman's voice asking for Ms Pagan Eliot. 'Speaking,' replied Pagan, quickly coming to the conclusion that it must be one of the other firms she had written to, then a deep masculine voice was coming out clearly, and the familiar tones left her in no doubt who was on the other end of the line.

She gripped the receiver till her knuckles showed white in a battle not to slam it down at once. It was a full moment before she could focus on what he was saying.

'—in the meantime I'd like you to have a look at the draft I've drawn up. If it meets with your approval we'll

get it drawn up properly, then all you need to do is sign
it——'

'Wait a minute,' she began weakly.

'Yes?'

Pagan paused. No, she was damned if she was going
to ask him to repeat what he'd just said as if she'd been
expecting a refusal, as if she expected to be punished for
her behaviour. She was in the right—had been all along.
And the fact that he was having legal documents drawn
up was tantamount to a confession of his own guilty
behaviour in all this.

'Nothing,' she said.

There was a pause from the other end.

'It's just that you seem to have got the solicitors
to move quite surprisingly quickly.' Her voice was
cool.

Was it her imagination, or was there a note of
disappointment in his voice?

'It's quite a simple procedure,' he told her, then with
a hint of steel coming into his tones, 'I'm glad to find
that you seem to have changed your mind about going
out of business. It'll be useful to have a Laser handy
whenever I need one.'

His cool took her breath away.

'I'm afraid I only hire them out to bone fide pupils,'
she told him primly.

'Perhaps in that case I could book in for a course of
lessons?'

'I'm sure there's nothing I can teach *you*,' she said as
rudely as she knew how.

Leale laughed pleasantly. 'I wouldn't say that. I'm
sure you have plenty of tricks up your sleeve.'

Pagan almost ground her teeth with rage, but her
voice was calm when she asked when she could expect
to see the draft agreement.

A change of subject was better than getting into
another verbal game of tennis when who knew what she
might find herself saying to him.

'I'm glad you asked about that,' he told her. 'Perhaps you would drop in tomorrow morning?'

It was more a statement than a request, and she was pleased to have a ready excuse on her lips.

'I'm afraid that's out of the question. I have a prior engagement,' she told him smoothly.

'Then what about lunch?'

'No, I-I couldn't do that,' she floundered, taken aback by the speed of his response.

'One o'clock would suit me very well. Here in the hotel, of course. Goodbye.' And before she could bring a croak of protest to her lips he had rung off.

'Well, of all the——' Pagan gazed, speechless, at the phone as if expecting it to burst into flames, and she had to fight not to pick it up and hurl it at the far wall.

Instead she lunged for the telephone directory and riffled through until she came to the list of hotels in the yellow pages at the back. It would be a minute's job to cancel the arrangement. And, said a warning voice, it would be a minute's job to trample underfoot the olive branch Leale was holding out to her. For the good of the school she would have to knuckle under to his arrogant, high-handed ways.

She let the phone directory slide from her grasp. This once, for this one last time, she would have to go along with what he wanted.

CHAPTER FIVE

THE suit was fine wool with a Liberty print border round the hem of the skirt in black, ivory, tan and cinnamon. There was a matching fringed shawl in the same colours. Pagan's chestnut hair was pinned on top of her head, and as a concession to Faynia she had smoothed on a little eye-shadow and blusher. With ten minutes or so before she need set off she inspected herself critically in the long mirror in her bedroom.

Faynia was right, the suit was her. Perhaps she wasn't sophisticated in the hard, glossy way of Leale de Laszlo's mistress, but she was groomed, well turned out, competent-looking.

Was she also, she wondered, with a little tightening feeling inside her stomach, the word he had used—stunning?

Mentally she kicked herself. What was she doing, caring about the way she looked for him? And wasn't all this bother about her appearance for him too? She didn't need to try to project any kind of glamour for her appointment with the representative from the company who might be willing to sponsor her. In fact, it would probably be a disadvantage to look too feminine. She wanted them to be convinced of her ability to tackle a tough assignment, and a too consciously feminine appearance would only confirm a prejudice that she would be unsuitable for something as tough as the Transatlantic.

She sighed. It was too late now to take down her hair and start again. She would simply have to convince them of her toughness right from the start.

She was in a fury when she drove out of the car park,

80

but it was no good driving in that state of mind, she told herself.

Mr Wilson, the promotions man, had turned out to be a short-legged, balding clone of Frank Sinatra—at least, if his toupee and his loosely knotted tie were anything to go by—and all she'd got from the encounter was in invitation to dinner and the information that a suitable craft was available, if someone, not them, could raise the asking price.

Pagan had declined the former and was dismayed by the latter.

With a superhuman effort she forced herself to calm down. Ahead of her was yet another arrogant male with a one-track mind and a load of problems for her. She put her foot down so that she was moving fast enough to have to focus all her concentration on the road ahead.

Owing to the delay caused by Wilson, she was twenty minutes late for her lunch date, and when she swung the battered old Renault into the forecourt car park the tall blond shape of Leale de Laszlo was visible through the open door inside the vestibule.

Pagan hadn't even had time to switch off the engine before he was loping, all tanned vigorous muscle, down the half-dozen steps from the porch, and by the time she was swinging her nylon-clad legs to the ground he was already holding open her car door.

She was irritated by such condescending male attention—as if she was a fragile doll incapable of opening her car door unaided! She began to regret the suit and the soft-fringed shawl and her hair, sleek and sophisticated, on top of her head. To compensate for it she edged him briskly away from the door and slammed it sportily behind her before turning towards him, legs slightly straddled like a tennis player waiting for return of serve.

But it was she who played the first shot. 'I haven't much time,' she told him without greeting. 'Can we get this damned thing signed straight away?'

Leale's expression didn't alter when he replied smoothly, 'I thought it would be more civilised to discuss it over a meal. I've had something laid on in my suite for us.'

'Discuss it? There's nothing to discuss, is there?' she replied rudely.

'I think you need to give yourself time to read the small print.'

'I intend to. But I don't think it need include a meal.'

'It's too late to cancel it now,' he told her.

'Then you'll just have to eat it all yourself,' Pagan retorted. Impatiently she added, because they hadn't moved from beside her car, 'Can we go in?'

Leale didn't move. 'I think we should come to some sort of consensus on the question of lunch before going inside. We can brawl with greater discretion out here.'

'I've no intention of brawling with you, either inside or out. I simply reserve my right to eat when and with whom I please!' She glared at him, braced for a fight.

Still he didn't move, merely regarding her levelly with those strange, sharply glittering pale eyes which seemed to be able to pierce right through her.

She felt her neck stiffen and she tossed her head with a show of nonchalance. 'Well?'

'I respect that right,' Leale told her equably after a long pause. 'And I'm sure you won't mind, then, if I choose to eat while we talk. My time is short and I may not have another opportunity until this evening.'

He turned abruptly and walked away without more ado, so that she had to run to keep up with him.

They approached the hotel entrance without another word being exchanged, but just before pushing the heavy carved door with his hand Leale turned, so suddenly that Pagan almost collided with him. At once he put out a hand to steady her, but she sidestepped nimbly and stood looking up at him with the light of battle still shining in her eyes.

'I take it that is your last word on lunch?' he asked, letting his hand drop.

She nodded. 'Of course. I'm very busy. I've already had to waste the morning in fruitless talk, and I don't intend to waste the afternoon as well. Besides,' she shot a look at him, 'I can't wait to get all this junk off and put on something comfortable again.'

She pulled at her shawl deprecatingly. Most men would at once have told her how marvellous she looked, but Leale merely looked her up and down as if he could quite see what she meant.

Unaccountably she felt piqued. 'Huh,' she thought, 'not up to the standard of his girl-friend, all paint and glamour!' And she glowered inside, trying to school her features into a mask of bored indifference.

'Take your shoes off when we get up stairs if your feet are killing you,' he threw back insultingly over his shoulder as he pushed on into the entrance hall.

His comment was calculated to make her feel like an ageing, crippled char. And when he disappeared inside, leaving her to follow behind and wrestle with the heavy wooden door by herself, she was not well pleased.

Briskly, as if taking her plea of haste to heart, he led her up a thickly carpeted side staircase to his suite. They went through some double doors and she found herself in what were obviously his own personal quarters. With the memory of her brush with Mr Wilson still fresh in her mind she hovered warily just by the doorway.

'Come in,' Leale called from a table by the window. 'Do you think I'm going to eat you? You can at least sit down.'

He indicated a chesterfield by the fireplace, but he himself took a seat at the table which was already laid for lunch by the window. He poured a glass of sherry, but Pagan shook her head. Before she had time to say anything else a door at the far end of the room opened and a waiter wheeled a trolley into the room. It was heavy with silver casseroles.

'I'm afraid only one of us is eating,' Leale told the waiter without even the flicker of a glance in Pagan's direction to see if at the sight and smell of food she had changed her mind.

'Very good, sir,' replied the waiter blandly. In a trice he had removed the place setting laid opposite Leale. 'Would the young lady like anything? Coffee, perhaps?' asked the waiter with a glance in her direction.

'No, thank you,' Pagan spoke up at once. 'I'm leaving shortly.'

The waiter inclined his head, then he was deftly heaping Leale's plate with an array of succulent-smelling food.

Pagan's mouth began to water, but she fixed her eyes stoically on the large ceramic pot in the fireplace with its artfully arranged dried grasses and wild flowers and tried not to remember the skimpy breakfast she had eaten that morning.

Without further preamble Leale began to eat as soon as the waiter left. Pagan tapped her foot impatiently on the floor as minutes passed and he gave no sign of obtaining the agreement for her to sign.

After a while she stole a glance at him. He was eating slowly and with obvious relish and as she watched he took a sip of wine. For an instant their eyes met, then he let his glance slide casually and deliberately back to his plate.

Pagan shifted in her seat. Her patience was at an end. But she dared not get on the wrong side of this man just yet, for he could easily smash her newly risen hopes if he so chose. Fortunately he spoke first.

'This is delicious,' he murmured, 'you should have had some.'

Pagan compressed her lips into a thin line of annoyance. 'Shall I have much longer to wait?' she demanded. 'Why the delay?'

'I expect they're getting round to it,' he replied with infuriating indifference. He seemed oblivious to the fact that she was beginning to fume.

'Would you mind telling them I'm in rather a hurry?' she demanded rudely.

'I expect they're doing their best,' he stonewalled. 'It is lunch-time, you know.' His tone was reproving and he added a slight smile with a raising of the eyebrows as if to say surely she didn't expect employees of his to go without lunch just because some unimportant girl claimed to be in a hurry. It was obvious, Pagan fumed inwardly, that he thought her time was less important than his own. Perhaps it was in terms of cash earned, but that didn't say anything about its value. Time was as valuable a commodity to her as it apparently was to him.

She stood up. 'Perhaps when they've managed to get it together you would kindly send me a copy through the post? If it's all right I'll sign it and put it in the post back again to you?' She picked up her bag.

Leale finished chewing before turning towards her. He raised his eyebrows. 'Oh, I don't think that would do,' he told her blandly. 'It seems you don't appreciate just how complicated these matters become once they're all tied up in legal jargon. I'd like to go over it paragraph by paragraph with you, just so I know you understand what you're putting your signature to. If you're really in so much of a hurry I can't keep you here, of course, but if you go now it will only mean that you'll have to come back some other day, and I'd have thought you wouldn't really want to do that.'

'You'd think right!' she retorted, unable to conceal her anger. 'Nor do I want to sit here and watch you eat. I can go to the zoo for that!' Her colour had risen and she clenched her fists.

'What do you suggest, then?' asked Leale, pointedly ignoring her insult like a rather bored parent speaking to a recalcitrant child. His equanimity only served to feed her wrath.

'I expect you to get the papers at once and let's get this thing sorted out once and for all!' she cried.

His only answer was to lean back in his chair and laugh softly. Pagan's cheeks burned with hot colour.

'You're insufferable!' she snarled, moving a step forward. 'Why are you playing with me like this? Is this how you always conduct your business? Is this how you treat your tenants?'

He sat up. 'My what?'

'Tenants, or whatever they are. You're supposed to deal in property, aren't you? What are you, some sort of Rachmann?' Her fists were still bunched by her sides, and she glared furiously across at him as if she would like nothing better than to wipe him out.

Leale continued to loll in his chair, however, with a half smile of amusement on his face. Dressed casually in cream trousers and a loose V-necked cricketing sweater he looked less intimidating than he had done in the business suit earlier in the week. Except for his infuriatingly complacent smile he looked almost approachable. Enticing, she thought, suddenly gasping for breath. Damn him, damn him! It was like a trap into which his unsuspecting victims willingly walked, while all he had to do was switch on the charm.

Pagan felt herself begin to tremble with impotent rage. He called the tune and he knew it. Short of walking out on him now in a flaming rage and putting the whole future of the school in jeopardy once again, she had no alternative but to curb her impatience and her fury, and, indeed, the violent demands of her self-esteem, and dance attendance on him until he saw fit to let the game come to an end.

Slowly he stood up and came from around the table towards her. When he was just a pace in front of her he stopped and held out a hand to her.

'Look,' he shrugged, 'I'm not playing cat and mouse with you. Business is business. I told them we'd be having something to eat before we needed to bother them. It's your own fault if you choose to starve yourself. I did tell you it would be lunch—I have to eat.

And I did wait for you. I'm not planning on a sybaritic repast going on all afternoon—I have work to do too. It was intended as a gesture of conciliation. We've both been behaving a little out of character, I suspect. And no, this isn't how I usually conduct business—but then I don't usually have business meetings with someone like you.'

'Back to that again!' Pagan's lip curled in derision. Almost up to his last words she had begun to feel her anger crumble under the accumulated self-doubt which his words seemed to activate, but now she knew she was on safe ground again. 'You try to belittle me all the time!' she stormed. 'If I was an ordinary businessman you wouldn't treat me like this!'

'Too true I wouldn't!' the devilish smile that broke across the levels of his handsome face was full of meaning.

'You——!' She lifted a hand in fury, but seeing the look in his eyes let it drop uselessly to her side.

His voice was soft. 'If you were an ordinary businessman, as you put it, I'd be cool and calm and rational.'

'Then be like that now!' she demanded angrily.

'Do you really want that?' Leale asked quietly.

'Why don't you treat me seriously?' she hissed in reply.

As if in answer he moved quickly towards her and before she knew what he was doing he had taken her by the forearms and turned her round to face the heavily decorated gilt mirror which hung over the marble fireplace.

Pagan struggled to release herself from his grasp, but he held her so closely to him that she knew it was hopeless to fight.

'Look,' he ordered huskily. 'What do you see there?'

Angrily she raised her face to the glass. Her hair was tousled now and her green eyes scowled sullenly back at her from out of the mirror. Over her shoulder she could

see, so close, too close, the strong tanned aristocratic
face of Leale de Laszlo. His eyes in the mirror were
looking straight into her own. Helplessly she tried to
struggle free, and in vain she watched as the blond head
bent inexorably to kiss the mouth of the girl turning
towards him in the mirror.

'You ask me to be cool and rational? I'm not
Superman,' he murmured huskily when at last he
released her. 'I've got the feelings and desires of any
man. Everything about you turns me on. I want you,
Pagan. How am I supposed to pretend you do nothing
to me?'

His hands started to roam her body, sending
shudders through her, and a thousand unbidden desires
danced before her.

His fair head bent to her again with a muffled groan.
It was not that her protests were unreal, but they were
vitiated by the growing fever in her blood, and despite
herself she felt her body mould itself to his. Her fingers
encircled his neck, seeking the living warmth of his
thick golden hair. And as he returned her kisses his lips
sought out the angle of her jaw, the hollow beneath her
ears, the smoothness of her neck down to her shoulders.

Her body responded wildly to the exploration of his
lips, but when he started to pull her blouse from the
waistband of her skirt to expose her bare midriff she
gave an exclamation of surprise.

It was only when his exploring fingers began to cup
her exposed breasts that in spite of the wild longing
their caress brought she struggled violently against him
and managed to draw back from him sufficiently to
break momentarily the spell he had begun to weave.

Heart pounding, Pagan leaned against him as if to
draw strength from the muscular virility of his form,
but when he tried to press the length of his body against
her own she managed to draw back again.

'No!' she breathed, almost in a swoon. 'This is
madness!' She staggered back, pushing the bottom of

her blouse back inside the waistband, running distraught fingers through her dishevelled hair, staring at him, eyes wide and vulnerable like those of a child. 'Please,' she whispered, 'please don't. It's not fair!'

'Pagan,' he coaxed, 'don't go away from me.' He came forward as if to take her in his arms again, but she backed away with a frightened look on her face. 'No!' she cried shakily.

'Why not?' he insisted. 'We want each other, why say no?'

Pagan backed farther off. Her voice, when she found it, was strained.

'Here? Now?' She tried to laugh. 'What sort of girl do you think I am?' Vainly she tried to still her heart, which was pounding now with anger as well as desire. 'How could you think I would. . . .' She looked round wildly for her things.

'Don't go yet.' Leale took her so gently into his arms that she forgot to resist and instead found herself, despite herself, succumbing to the now quite different caress of his fingers through her tumbled hair.

He kept quite still, holding her so tightly that she could hear his heart thumping in his chest, but she felt the burning imprint of his hard-muscled body begin to stir hers to an even greater renewal of response. Unable to move away, she lay in his arms while his fingers remained looped in her chestnut hair and he buried his face in the coils of her unpinned tresses for a long delicious nerve-tingling moment without moving.

'Pagan, Pagan,' he murmured at last, raising his head so that he could look straight into her eyes. 'Won't you live up to your name for me?' He brushed her lips. 'I want you, girl. And it may have escaped your notice, but I always get what I want. Don't even try to resist me, because I know that you want me too.'

She strove to control the heady mixture of feelings that assailed her and, head thrown slightly back, she looked up, not yet conquered, full into his eyes.

'Maybe you've never met your match before,' she breathed, her eyes flashing with a strange green fire. 'Perhaps I'm not of the same breed as the women you're used to. . . .'

He laughed softly as her words trailed away as he brought her close once again. 'That's true—so true. You're on your own. But you know you want me as much as I want you, whatever breed of woman you are.'

Pagan shuddered. She was being asked to do something she had never done before, to surrender her common sense to the overwhelming inferno of irrational desire.

She shook her head, but she moved as if mesmerised in his arms. Only a hard inner core of resolution made her eyes gleam with the singleness of her conviction. 'They have their own rules for living. I have mine,' she told him, trying to bring a note of firmness into her voice.

He began to laugh softly again. 'My Pagan,' he chided, 'I do believe you're scared!'

'Scared?'

'Of me.'

'Rot!' She pulled away in an almighty effort to break his spell and as calmly as she knew how she began to pick up her things. 'I'm afraid of nothing whatever,' she announced. And, more convincingly, 'Nothing and no one frightens me!'

Leale watched her for a moment with an amused smile on his face before coming to her once again and taking her bag out of her hand and placing it on the chair beside them.

'Let's finish our official business, then we can talk.'

Caught, she could only shrug agreement.

He went to a bell push in the wall and rang it. Then he turned to her. 'Are you sure you won't have anything to eat?'

'Quite,' she retorted, forcing herself not to look longingly at the still spread succulence of the meal.

He poured her a glass of wine. 'Here, at least try this. It's rather special.'

Pagan sipped the wine while trying to avoid his eyes. They seemed to be on her all the time, laughing, blue, bright as crystal and as sharp. She felt skewered as if he could pick her up and inspect her at will, and she began to blush under his scrutiny.

'Which is the real you,' he asked at last, 'the sophisticated woman in the high heels and sheer nylons, or the gamine, playing pirates out in the bay?'

'You're the pirate!' she broke out before she could stop herself.

He stood erect, hands in pockets, bronzed, hawklike countenance expressing authority in every line, eyes sailor-blue now with amusement.

'Tell me why you're all togged up in this gear if you don't like it,' he asked easily, lolling down on to the arm of the chair beside her and grinning at her so irresistibly that she found it almost impossible to restrain the sudden impulse to go to him and let her lips wander intimately over his smooth jaw and into the hollows of his cheeks and eyes.

She forcibly concentrated on the pattern of the chair cover behind him. 'I had a meeting,' she told him grudgingly. 'So-called sponsors.'

Then, in a rush of feeling, she told him about her morning.

He listened without saying anything, but there was an alternation of anger and deep thought in his eyes throughout her story. When she finished with a rueful little shrug he sighed and pulled himself upright to stand at the window with his back to her for a moment or two. Then he swung round to give her a long, searching look. All her muscles tensed as he came towards her, but he merely took her empty wine glass from her. 'I'm sorry,' he told her unexpectedly, 'all that to go through and then me. You know I'm not a cheap joker like that, don't you?' He shrugged and gave a lopsided grin. 'But who knows? Maybe that is how you see me?' His glance was sharp when he looked into her eyes. 'You'll have to make up your own mind about that. I'm not going to hide from you the kind of life I lead. I'm never in one place for long. I like female companionship and,' he shrugged deprecatingly, 'women seem to like me. Or my money.'

He grinned. 'They know the score. No hearts are broken.'

When he looked carefully into her face she was unable to guess what was on his mind. But she said, 'I'm never going to be that sort of woman, ever.' She felt a shudder go through her body which told her that he was right. She did want him.

She stiffened. She wanted him—but not on those terms. Never on those terms.

Leale seemed to understand, for he took her gently in his arms and, pushing her tangled hair from her brow, kissed her solemnly on the forehead.

'Pax,' he said. 'I promise I'll never try to get you to do anything against your will. But,' he added devilishly, 'that doesn't mean I shan't try to change your will!'

Pagan let herself relax in his arms for a moment. A wish flared briefly that he didn't have to be quite so ruggedly handsome, quite so outrageously masculine, but before she could quash the flicker of desire which arose at the same time, the door flew open at the far end of the apartment and a girl burst into the room.

'Darling!' she warbled, then stopped, her scarlet mouth with its exaggerated cupid's bow dropping open in astonishment.

Pagan felt Leale's fingers relax their hold round her waist a little, but he didn't let her go at once. Instead he turned easily towards the woman with an amused smile playing across his face.

'Michelle!' he exclaimed without a trace of surprise, 'I rang through to the office just now. Where is everyone? We're waiting for that bit of paper from the solicitors.'

Michelle stood in the doorway, hand on hip. For an instant her face showed the trace of a petulant scowl as she swept Pagan from head to foot, but she covered the look at once, opening big blue eyes in mock astonishment at the girl even now standing within the circle of Leale's arms.

'Why, darling, I didn't realise you were still busy!'

Somehow she managed to imbue the last word with an insulting innuendo, and Pagan felt a flash of colour rise in her cheeks.

Leale laughed easily. 'Just run along, there's a sweetie, and find out what's happened, would you?' Couched though the request was in terms of endearment, it was unmistakably an order. But the girl had no intention of running along anywhere, and she made it clear by undulating right into the room towards them. Her arms were full of what looked like different fabric samples and she wore a purple knitted dress which left nothing to the imagination. She was obviously bra-less, for it clung so tightly to her form that her pert nipples were clearly outlined and the wool was stretched tight over the taught curve of her buttocks. She came towards Leale, for her eyes were only for him, with a sultry smile on her face, then she bent down to place the samples on the chair beside them.

She had her back to him and instead of straightening up immediately she made some excuse to remain bending like that while she looked back at him with a provocative smile from beneath heavily mascaraed lashes.

'Look what I've got,' she said, in her little-girl voice, 'all the samples you asked for.'

Pagan noted that Leale's glance had now alighted on the girl's provocatively curved behind and she pulled herself away from him with disgust at such a blatant attempt at seduction, and at the man for so obviously relishing it.

Leale, however, squeezed her waist and pulled her

back to him. His eyes never left Michelle. 'You have been a busy woman,' he replied meaningfully.

Pagan tried again to move out of his grasp. She felt like someone prying through a keyhole, and the last thing she wanted was to see inside Leale's life if it contained such scenes as this, but his grip was unshakeable.

'Now would you mind doing as I've just asked?' There was no note of anger in his voice, but there was a steel which brooked no further argument.

Michelle, however, was not to be so easily dislodged from her position. She sat down on the chesterfield and lay back with her arms outstretched the better to display herself to his gaze. She allowed his eyes to travel slowly over her body, making sure he was taking in every slinky curve, every jutting line, then she opened her scarlet mouth to laugh softly, wriggling her body inside the purple dress and throwing back her head in a simulation of surrender.

'But, darling,' she purred, 'you said it was urgent. I've moved heaven and earth to gather the samples for you so quickly. I thought we had to choose the curtain fabrics first? An old manor house like that will take a lot of time and care if we're going to restore it properly.'

Pagan took advantage of Leale's concentration on the blonde to slide free of his restraining arm. Once again she picked up her bag.

A gleam of triumph shone momentarily in the blue eyes of the girl in purple. It was quickly dispelled, however, by the cold glance Leale shot in her direction when he told her, 'I'm busy now. I'll look at them later this afternoon in the office.'

Michelle obviously knew when it was worth pushing her interests and when it was more prudent to appear to comply with his wishes, for with a little-girl pout, she snaked herself upright and stood up as if to go. But before leaving she made it clear that she was not

defeated by going over to him and planting a little
flirtatious kiss on his cheek. Her dark eyelashes
fluttered like trapped moths and her lip-gloss left a
small red brand on his smooth skin as if to say, this is
mine. Then the door closed behind her.

Pagan had somehow brought her galloping heart
under control. She let out a long, silent breath and
raised her eyes coolly to his. 'That shade doesn't do
much for you,' she remarked flippantly, indicating the
trace of glosser left on his face.

Leale took a handkerchief from his pocket and
dabbed ineffectually at the brand. 'Would you do it for
me?' he murmured, moving to her.

She looked back at him coldly, her heart beating a
wild syncopation of despair, but her voice was steady
when it came. 'I'm sure a big, strong man like you can
remove the traces of his girl-friend's lipstick efficiently
enough if he sets his mind to it.'

She turned away abruptly, every line in her body
designed to show a cutting derision which did not
express all of her true feelings at that moment, but she
played out the charade with determination, regarding
Leale coolly through the mirror where not ten minutes
before she had watched, hypnotised, as his lips had
come down to claim her own.

She saw him move towards her now as if to take her
in his arms again, but she slid casually away to take up
a position by the window.

Before he could remonstrate, Michelle had returned
with the papers. She posted herself on the chesterfield
again while Leale rapidly went through the details with
a Pagan whose mind seemed numb now with the events
which had just gone before. All the time he spoke she
was conscious of the nearness of his lithe, muscled
body, of the tang of his skin with its faint perfume of
some expensive aftershave, of the fire still smouldering
in her body. But she was tortured too by the awareness
of Michelle's eyes on her, watching, assessing, gauging

reactions, and of the other woman's deliberate, almost spoken warning, that this man was her property.

Miserably Pagan nodded when he asked if she understood the documents. She would read it all properly later. What did it matter, what did any of it matter now? As long as they could use the lane she didn't care what subclause 3(d) said.

She nodded again. Hating, the man, hating the woman, hating herself even more for being such a naïve and gullible little fool.

Why, oh, why had she got herself involved in a set-up like this?

Why oh why had she allowed such a dreadful pair to drive her to such an extremity of feeling?

So oppressed was she by the presence of them both that she picked up the pen Leale had taken out and abruptly asked him, 'Where do I sign?'

Surprise showed itself for a moment, but she bent her head and carefully wrote her name in the space he indicated.

'So that's that.' She raised her clouded eyes to him. Now we need never meet again, she thought dully. She got up to go. She did it so briskly that she was at the door before Leale realised she meant it.

At that moment Michelle squealed, 'Oh, look, darling, this is the one—look!'

Momentarily distracted, Leale turned back to say something.

It was enough. In a trice Pagan was through the door and had closed it firmly behind her before he could say another word.

CHAPTER SIX

HEART in her mouth, Pagan had hurried down the lushly carpeted corridor to the same side-stairs up which she had been led earlier. It was with relief that she stepped outside into the cool clear sunlight of the gardens. A strong scent of something sharp like mint filled the air, and she took in deep gulping breaths as if to rid herself of something unwholesome in the atmosphere of the hotel.

I should be happy, she told herself, clutching the deeds to her chest. I should be happy. This is a red-letter day for the school.

She got the door of her car open quickly and slipped into the driver's seat. It was a moment before she started the engine. Almost fearing to, she turned her head once in the direction of the hotel. The drive, the steps, the vestibule, or what she could still see of it, remained empty.

She let out a breath to ease the tension. So that was that? She was free. She gunned the car into life and made off as rapidly as possible up the drive to the main road and home.

When she eventually reached the boathouse, she decided to ring Tim and Jan straightaway to share the good news.

'Well, some of it's good,' she was telling Jan a few moments later, 'the stuff about the right of way, but I'm afraid I drew a blank on the sponsorship issue. All they did really was give me the name of a boatbuilder with a possible craft. I suppose I may as well go out to have a look at it. But it'll have to be after the weekend, as we seem to be fully booked up again.'

'At least that's something to be cheerful about,'

replied Jan. 'And you never know, this boat may be exactly what you want.'

'That would only rub salt in the wound,' answered Pagan. 'What's the use of a boat without the money to buy it with?'

'True,' she agreed, 'but you never know, something may turn up soon. Keep trying, that's the important thing.'

'By the way, how do you feel about working this weekend?' asked Pagan, pleased to be able to turn the conversation onto something less problematical.

'I'm fit as two fiddles,' laughed Jan. 'But I've got some news for you.'

'Oh?' Pagan was intrigued by the note of suppressed excitement in Jan's voice.

'Can't you guess?' the older woman asked.

Pagan hesitated. 'It's obviously something good.'

'That depends on one's point of view,' responded Jan quickly. 'It has its awkward aspects, coming at this time.' She paused. 'Pagan, sit down a minute—listen, I'm going to have a baby!'

Pagan was stunned. She had known Tim and Jan for such a long time and had got into the habit of thinking of the two of them as a unit, complete in themselves. Indeed they were almost like brother and sister to her, and, she thought, to each other. It would take some readjustment to think of them as a family unit now.

'I'm so happy for you,' she told her. 'Is Tim pleased?'

Jan laughed. 'He pretended to be cross at first. After all, it spoils our five-year plan. We hadn't scheduled in a family for another year to eighteen months—that's the time he'd estimated it would take for the sailing school to get itself right off the ground and provide all of us with a comfortable living. Like most men, though, he's been going around with a broad grin on his face ever since the idea really struck home. He can't wait to start wheeling the pram. But Pagan,' her voice held a note of caution, 'we only found out yesterday and he doesn't want anybody but you and close family to know just yet.' She laughed. 'I told him, if you go waltzing into school with that look on your face you might as well carry a badge and poster as well!' She laughed again, contentedly. 'I still haven't got used to the idea myself. It all seems as if it's happening to somebody else. I'm starting pre-natal classes next week, so no doubt that will bring me down to earth.'

Pagan wondered if she should broach the question of Jan's continued employment as a sailing instructor just yet, but the problem was taken out of her hands when Jan herself said: 'It's fortunate in some respects that it's happened now. It seems I shan't be too gross to sail the dinghies this season; in fact the elephantine stage will only happen when the season is over. Tim was impressed by my timing. I hope you are.'

'I'm relieved,' admitted Pagan. 'Instructors as dependable as you are hard to find. Boys are ten a penny, but they're a bit here-today-gone-tomorrow at that age, and it's nice to have a couple of older allies to rely on once the season gets into its vicious stage. Are you sure you'll be able to cope, though? What about morning sickness or whatever they call it?'

'I'll be O.K.,' Jan reassured her. 'I've always been pretty fit. No need to worry.'

After a few more words she rang off and Pagan went up to her bedroom to change.

Jan had said she would let Tim know about the boat that had been recommended to her and they would all arrange to go up together to have a look at it. There was no harm in looking, thought Pagan, and somehow it made her ambition that little bit more tangible.

She had just taken off the Liberty wool suit and was wearing nothing but a pair of lacy knickers when the phone rang.

'Hello,' came a familiar voice. 'You were on the phone a long time!'

She could think of no immediate retort.

'Hello, are you there?' he asked.

'Leale, what do you want?'

'Don't sound so troubled! You ran out on me again, didn't you? I've already told you, no one ever does that to me.'

'I did not "run out" as you put it, I merely left when we seemed to have concluded our business.'

'But no way had we concluded it——' he interrupted. 'It was just getting interesting. I was beginning to feel for the first time that I was really getting to know you.'

'Hold the line a moment.'

Whether he would or not she put the receiver down on the bed and went to pick up a wrap. Then, without hurrying, she slipped on a pair of warm slippers.

'That's better,' she told him coolly when she returned. 'I was just getting changed when you rang. It's too cold to stand around with nothing on at this time of year.'

'Are you properly dressed now?' he chuckled.

'Yes, thank you,' Pagan replied primly.

'I wish I was there to undress you again,' he told her in lazily suggestive tones.

She was glad he couldn't see the blush which came to her cheeks.

'Are you ringing for any particular reason?' she demanded, 'or merely passing the time of day? As I've already told you, I am rather busy.'

Her voice was deliberately hard as ice. But despite that she heard him laugh pleasantly.

'Well now,' he began, 'I felt like hearing the sound of your voice, the friendly notes floating over the line.'

'Now you've heard it it'll be in order for me to ring off without being accused of running out on you, will it?' she taunted.

'No, don't ring off yet, Pagan,' his voice pleaded. 'There was something I wanted to say, but just hearing your voice has sent it right out of my mind.'

'I'm sure you're not as easily disconcerted as that,' she jibed.

'You'd be surprised! My heart is beating double rate, my hands are shaking, and I'm coming out in a fine sweat, all because I'm afraid you'll put the receiver down before I've finished.'

'You're very plausible,' she matched his irony, 'but I'm afraid you'll have to try harder than that.'

'I'm doing my best—have pity on me!'

Pagan sighed. 'I really mean it. I shall have to go.'

She didn't know why he'd bothered to ring; her words weren't designed to provoke a dinner invitation from him. But as soon as they were out of her mouth she realised how it would sound to someone like him, so she had an answer on her lips.

His words, however, came as a surprise. He said, 'I'd like to counter the impression you have of me as some kind of super-swine landlord, turning innocent people out of their homes. That's not my game at all.'

'You've no need to worry,' she replied coldly. 'I really haven't time to speculate on your business affairs, surprising though it may seem to you. Now if you'll excuse me, I must get on.'

And with that she firmly and unhurriedly replaced the receiver.

The phone didn't ring again as she'd half expected and she had no idea why Leale had bothered to ring merely in order to make excuses for himself, if indeed that was the real reason for his call. Whatever the case, she felt she had won a minor victory by being so firm.

'He surely couldn't care less what *I* think of him,' she told Faynia when they met up later that evening at Renoir's. 'His opinion of himself is good enough to satisfy anybody's ego. What odds does it make if I think badly of him? Anyway,' she morosely swirled the ice in her glass before looking across the table at her friend, 'at least we've settled the right of way.'

Faynia kept glancing towards the door.

'What are you trying to tell me?' asked Pagan when

she intercepted the last of these looks. 'Is *he* about to
arrive?'

'Yes. And I'm wondering if it's too soon for you and
him to meet casually just yet.'

'At least you're honest. But you don't expect me to
leave, do you?'

Faynia grimaced. 'He hasn't mentioned you for a
couple of days.'

'There you are, then,' put in Pagan at once, not at all
put out.

'But who knows what deep, secret hurt he's
harbouring in the deepest recesses of his soul?' Faynia
giggled.

'Don't you take anything seriously?' demanded
Pagan. 'You asked me to move over, to sacrifice the
love of my life in order to further your ambitions, and
now you're being frivolous about him.'

She could play Faynia's game. Both girls giggled,
then Faynia tried to pull a straight face.

'We only joke about what lies closest to our hearts,'
she primly informed her friend.

'*You* might.' Pagan got up. 'We're not all tarred with
the same brush. Anyway, I see my date for the evening,'
she said.

Faynia swivelled her head. 'That *boy*?'

Pagan pretended to be hurt. 'He's a year older than
me. Just because I employ him it doesn't put him out of
bounds.'

Faynia stretched languidly, '*Chacun à son goût*,' she
said. 'Perhaps we'll all meet up later?'

Pagan went over to Bobby with a grin. He wasn't her
date, not in any real sense, but she had bumped into
him that afternoon and after chatting amicably for a
while he had casually suggested meeting later for a
drink. He was the most amusing of the instructors,
always ready for a bit of horseplay, but as serious and
competent as any of them when necessary. Now she
looked forward to the evening as a bit of welcome light

relief from the storms and unexpected passions of that morning.

'What would you like to drink?' were his first words as she came up to him.

Guiltily realising that it was money she herself had paid him for his previous weekend's work, she asked for a half of cider and jokingly told him that she hoped he wasn't going to go all male chauvinist on her and insist on paying all evening.

'Not if you protest loudly enough,' he joked.

When he came back with the drinks to their booth he said seriously enough, 'You don't look like one of those tough Women's Libbers.'

'One doesn't have to be covered in six inches of muscle with a face like tanned leather to want to have the right to be able to stand up for oneself,' she told him. 'Everybody should feel free to make up their own minds how they want to live. Nobody should be forced to give up something they enjoy just because it's not ladylike—or not masculine,' she added. 'It works both ways.'

'I think you're terrific, Pagan,' he blurted suddenly. 'Best boss I've ever had.'

She blushed at the unexpected innocence of his tribute, but before she could think of a reply, he had taken her hand and was dragging her to her feet.

'Come on, let's have a bop!'

She allowed him to march her out on to the little dance floor.

It was fun being with Bobby. He seemed full of a puppy-like enthusiasm and energy. After dancing for a while Pagan felt her cares beginning to lift. Between numbers she began to tell him about the right of way, and when she finished he hugged her spontaneously. 'That's wonderful!' he cried.

His enthusiasm was catching. She hugged him back, and it was just at that moment that she raised her head and found herself looking straight into a pair of glittering eyes that sent a shudder of apprehension through her. Leale de Laszlo smiled sardonically when their eyes met. He raised his glass to her.

Confused, Pagan turned away, averting her head as if to say something to her partner. Bobby's arms were still loosely enfolding her and he felt her stiffen.

'What's the matter?' he asked attentively.

'Talk of the devil,' she said. 'There he is—the man who's had our lives in his hands all week.'

Bobby glanced across the crowded dance floor and a smile broke across his face.

'That's great!' he pronounced unexpectedly. 'I didn't realise it was him. He's a real character. He was chatting to me the other day on the foreshore, while you were teaching that young Robinson kid.'

Pagan sniffed. Bobby's enthusiasm was almost disloyal!

He looked down at her. 'Don't you approve of him, then?' he asked.

Pagan pulled a face, and Bobby's response was to pull her a little closer to him.

'I thought he was the heart-throb type, the kind all women go for,' he bantered.

'Some might,' shrugged Pagan. 'He leaves me cold. I don't find arrogance a particularly endearing trait.'

She turned as a hand touched her shoulder and found she was being pressed up close against the lean body of Leale de Laszlo himself as the crowd began to surge off the small dance floor between numbers. The look on his face told her that it was no accident that his body was pressing against hers, as if accidentally brought close by the crowd. But Bobby, perhaps encouraged by her judgment, still had his arm loosely but proprietorially around her shoulders.

For a brief instant Leale's face was very close to her own. She knew without a shadow of a doubt that he had overheard what she had been saying.

Coolly she looked up into his eyes. 'Slumming tonight,

are we?' she asked bitingly. Then, not waiting for a reply, she turned back to Bobby and snuggled into his arms. The boy responded by putting his other arm arm around her waist so that her back was turned to Leale.

It was such a calculated brush-off that she wasn't surprised when she felt Leale move on past them. It was only the silly lisping sound of a woman's voice shrieking, 'Darling, let's get out of this dreadful crush!' that made her crane her neck round Bobby's shoulders to catch sight of Michelle simpering up into Leale's rather bored-looking face.

She just had time to see the blonde's scarlet talons slide into the lush hair at the back of Leale's neck before Bobby was turning her expertly on to the dance floor. Then the music, loud and mindlessly jolly, seemed to crash into her ears, mocking the sudden sick feeling that seemed to threaten to engulf her.

They danced, it seemed, for hours, with the music apparently never-ending, and because it was a Friday night, the place was packed to the doors with people determined to enjoy themselves.

Unused to such places, Pagan felt lightheaded with the heat, the noise, the flashing coloured lights and the continually gyrating sticky bodies on all sides.

Despite Michelle's words they did not leave, and Pagan was subjected to the sight of them dancing together in such a way that she was left in no doubt as to their relationship. Not that a casual observer would have thought little different at the sight of her and Bobby. It was impossible to avoid physical contact in all that crush, even if she had wanted to, and there was even a sort of comfort in the brotherly closeness of his fit young body. It was a novel experience for Pagan to be out dancing with a crowd of people the same age as herself too, and she blamed only herself for being unable to enjoy things wholeheartedly.

Bobby drew her into a quietish corner eventually and gave her a searching look.

'Are you tired, Pagan? You look a little strained.'

'No,' she replied at once, touched by his concern.

She was shocked to realise that tears were suddenly very close. To hide them and save herself the embarrassment of explanations she rested her forehead on his shoulder. He patted her and gently began to stroke her hair with his free hand.

'You are tired,' he told her. 'I don't mind if you want to go.' Then she felt him turn a little. 'Goodnight!' he called to someone.

'Who was that?' She asked without raising her face.

'Your de Laszlo man,' he told her, not realising how he was twisting the knife, 'and that amazing blonde bird of his. Sorry,' he checked himself. He squeezed Pagan's shoulder. 'She looks like a model. Rather out of place in this part of the world, don't you think?'

He held her close in a comfortable sort of way for a moment or two, while Pagan's thoughts plodded dully around the cause of her pain. At last, with a resolute lift of her head, she found herself able to smile up at him. 'Let's go, then!' With sudden resolution she began to move towards the exit. She was an idiot to feel hurt by him. He'd been playing with her all along. The fact that she couldn't cope with the feelings he aroused in her confirmed that she was out of his league. Yes, he was strictly offside.

Arm-in-arm, she and Bobby made their way up the stairs to street level. With a strange feeling that it had all happened before, Pagan noticed that Leale's big white foreign convertible was parked across the kerb and he was leaning nonchalantly against the hood as if waiting for someone as they came out on to the street.

He looked up and gave them both a charmingly polite smile.

'Hi. Had a good time?' he asked Bobby.

The younger man was obviously pleased at being recognised and he stopped for a moment. It was long enough for Leale to tell him, 'Michelle's forgotten something. We were just wondering if there was anywhere to go on to for a drink, but it seems not. Would you care to come back to my hotel for a nightcap?'

To Pagan's dismay Bobby had accepted before she could think up an excuse.

'But tomorrow morning I have to——' she began to protest weakly.

'The night's still young,' Leale grinned. 'Live for the moment!'

Still protesting, she saw Leale turn back deliberately to Bobby and engage him in some chat about sailing, then Michelle emerged from the club and entwined herself possessively around Leale's neck.

Pagan allowed herself to go numb. There was no point in feeling anything; it was all pain. She watched the three of them as if they were actors on a stage and she was powerless to intercede.

It was in that mood that she heard Michelle ask, 'Are we all going in our car, or are you going to follow?' She addressed Bobby who, having come on his motor-bike grinned and shrugged.

Pagan quickly said she would prefer to drive. Bobby would come with her. Perhaps alone in the car she could plead a headache and get out of the invitation.

Then Leale spoke up as if to settle the matter. 'We'll all go in my car.' Pagan noticed he had subtly reclaimed sole ownership. 'I'll bring you back into town afterwards to pick up your respective vehicles.'

His tone of voice told her that he would brook no further argument. Pagan felt like one of the massed poor the way she was being organised, but there was no time to dwell on it. In a moment they were enveloped in the dim luxury of the huge car. The stereo was turned low, surrounding them in the heartrending sounds of late-night schmaltz. It was just the kind of yearning ballad to bring tears for what might-have-been to her eyes. She leaned her head back against the voluptuously upholstered seat and tried to douse the fire in her blood. In that position Bobby found it hard to put his arm round her and had to content himself with a little silent hand-holding. Moreover, without realising it, she had placed herself so that she could see the clean-cut lines of Leale's face in the driving mirror as if to add to her pain. Uselessly she tried to drag her glance from the taunting image of his face, but when his eyes left the road for a minute and met hers in the glass her heart did a double-somersault and she found it impossible to tear her glance from his.

Wretchedly she felt herself being drawn into a game of cat and mouse which only ended when he swung the car in front of the hotel and brought it to a standstill. With the engine off he turned round in his seat and they looked at each other without the intermediary of the mirror. There was no need to speak; something passed between them faster and more eloquent than mere words. But Michelle broke the spell with her childish babble and by the time Leale had come round the car to open her door for her Pagan had managed to retrieve something of her self-control.

She avoided any contact with him when they went inside the hotel, and with its discreet lighting by means of ornate Victorian wall-lights, they seemed to move through the shadows like wraiths. All except Michelle. She at least made no attempt to be quiet. They went up to Leale's apartment in the lift, and as soon as the door closed Michelle wriggled provocatively against Leale, but she was saying something teasing to Bobby at the same time, her eyes calculating beneath thick lashes.

Leale caught Pagan's eye over the blonde head and there seemed to be a faint smile lurking in eyes which Pagan had come to learn already gave nothing away unless they wanted to. She turned her own head slightly in disapproval, but Bobby was smiling at Michelle and she felt she was beginning to lose her only ally.

With trepidation she followed everyone out and trod the short distance to the familiar double doors which led to Leale's apartment. With a sickening jolt she heard Michelle, as she swept grandly into the room beyond.

'They've done us proud, haven't they, Bobby?' She stretched her arms out proprietorially to take in the rich furnishings of the elegant gold and white room, and, thought Pagan darkly, her gesture was intended to include the rooms beyond, rooms which would contain no doubt only one bed.

Leale caught her look. 'So dark and subdued tonight,' he murmured, caressing her with his glance.

'You say *I'm* territorial,' she muttered, glancing at the other girl.

'I wasn't comparing, merely describing,' he averred. 'Would you deny it?'

Pagan scowled, unable to help herself. Of course he was right: she was feeling territorial about him, hence her present pain. But the last thing she was going to do was agree with him.

'I'd deny it,' she said emphatically.

'Good,' he replied smoothly, 'because I think there's going to be a take-over bid for something of yours very shortly.'

She followed his glance and took in the scene on the sofa with only mild concern. Bobby, it seemed, had been picked to star in a scene with Michelle as his opposite number. She hadn't actually started to unbutton his shirt yet, but her hands were all over him, teasing, provoking, making him laugh, playing with him, so that his inexperience glared out at them all. Pagan was embarrassed for him. Michelle had started on the Bacardi as soon as they had entered the room, but even the empty glass beside him was no excuse for his inept fencing with the girl, experienced in this sort of thing as she obviously was.

'You really don't mind?' asked Leale.

There was something gentle in his voice which made her look up.

'Of course not,' she told him. 'He'll no doubt feel, rather awkward in front of his boss tomorrow morning,' she tried to laugh lightly.

'His boss?' Leale looked puzzled.

'Me,' she told him succinctly.

Something which could easily have masqueraded as relief seemed to come into his eyes. 'I thought maybe he was your steady date,' he murmured. 'In which case I might have stepped in before it reached round ten. However, if it's all right with you, I think we can safely leave them to it. There are far more interesting things to talk about, don't you think?'

Michelle's little-girl laugh floated across the room.

'Don't *you* mind?' demanded Pagan. 'She's supposed to be your property, isn't she? If you will insist on looking at people in that way.'

'She's a free agent,' he told her, 'and so am I.' He gave a short, hard laugh. 'One thing we must get straight, Pagan—no one owns me, and I'll respond to that by not putting any false restrictions on the women I'm involved with.'

'That sounds very neat. Especially when by involvement you mean a purely physical one. Who would want to make that a basis for anything more binding?'

She let a little smile of derision play across her face. 'You'd no doubt sing a different tune if you really cared about someone.'

The expression on Leale's face didn't tell her anything. 'Perhaps,' was all he would concede. He took her hand, and she felt like a captive, without any will of her own. Only the proximity of Michelle and Bobby on the chesterfield seemed to be able to save her from the numbness that seemed to creep up her spine.

She watched, fascinated, as Leale raised the hand which she supposed was hers to his lips. 'It's no good now,' she told him dully. 'I can't feel anything.'

It was all wrong, what she was saying. It only made him chuckle and press his lips again and again on to the back of her hand, then inch by inch up the inside of her arm.

'Just think what you'll be missing,' he murmured, slowly drawing her towards him.

In gradually mounting horror and shame Pagan felt him slip his hand underneath her T-shirt, then he was bringing his lips burningly down on to her exposed breasts.

'No!' she moaned, torn by the red-hot waves of desire that surged over her, and the thought of Bobby or even Michelle raising their heads at any moment to look over the back of the sofa. Her quick glance across the room told her that Bobby at least had his mind on other things, and Leale, quick to interpret her look, murmured between kisses, 'We'll go to my room if you prefer a little more privacy.'

It was at this point that Pagan realised she should say no and mean it, but the word would not speak itself. Passively she allowed him to lead her through one of the far doors. All the while his hands were caressing her naked skin to a state of fevered pleasure and his lips, light and warm, and full of knowledge, sought out the most intimate parts of her breasts.

He had already started to unzip the front of her jeans when something like a bomb exploded in her mind. Here she was, being dragged off to the bedroom of some man, almost a stranger, like any cheap tart he might pick up in a hotel. Though, she had time to think, the tarts in this hotel would no doubt be anything but cheap!

Sickened, she tried to pull her T-shirt back into place. Twisting and turning, she struggled out of his restraining arms and panting a little with the exertion backed away from him, her eyes dark with humiliation.

'I'm not like this,' she groaned, running a hand through her tousled hair.

'Are you trying to tell me you're nothing but a little tease?' Leale lunged for her, dragging her tightly back against his hard body.

'You brought me here—you practically kidnapped me! I had no choice. It's you who made assumptions about my amenability——'

'That's a long word for this time of night.' He wasn't really listening, one hand was already busy with the zipper of her jeans while the other pinned her roughly against his muscled body. In a trice he had his hands inside the fine lace of her panties, caressing the soft flesh of her buttocks, kneading and drawing her now unresisting beneath him. Pagan felt his weight topple her slowly back on to something soft in the darkened room, and worse, she felt her body arch against his with the power of its animal need.

From side to side her head twisted in a frenzy with the vain attempt to avoid his searching lips, but it only seemed to act as a spur to his pleasure, for he gave a little moan under his breath and she felt his mouth move hotly down the length of her, questing in sensuous delight for the most intimate parts of her body.

'I'm not like this,' she cried again and again. 'Let me go, please, Leale!'

He laughed deep in his throat and rolled her over so that he could pull her jeans from under her.

'I've never done this before—please don't,' she pleaded.

She felt his head raise itself from its play on the skin at the small of her back and his hands gripped her round the waist with unaccustomed brutality.

'Don't please, don't,' she wept. 'I don't know what to do. Please Leale, let me go!'

CHAPTER SEVEN

Something in her voice made him hesitate. Slowly, very slowly, he dragged his body up till it covered hers. Then both of his hands slid one to each breast and she felt his hard muscled strength relax.

His voice when it came close behind her ear was hoarse with emotion. 'Are you trying to tell me you're a virgin, Pagan?'

She nodded, hot tears of anger and humiliation all at once pouring from her eyes.

He moved her over so that she lay half facing him in his arms.

'Why on earth didn't you say before this?' he demanded harshly.

'Maybe you'd have preferred it if I'd worn a badge?' she retorted, scrubbing at the tears in her eyes.

'That would have saved a lot of trouble,' he replied, allowing his lips to move provokingly down her wet cheek to the hollow of her neck. 'I suppose it means you take no precautions of any sort?' he muttered, still busy at her neck.

She tried to push his head with its heavy shock of fair hair away, without success.

'I take the best precaution of all,' she retorted. 'I say "no".'

'It's not doing you much good tonight.'

'Most men,' she responded tartly, 'are not heels.'

'I wouldn't bet on it,' quipped Leale, briefly raising his head. He looked down at her tear-stained face. 'Actually, you're in luck, because neither am I—a heel, I mean.'

He rolled away from her with a slight groan.

'Whether you accept this or not,' he told her, 'you've

led me on right from the start. Everything you've done, the way you've looked at me, the way you speak to me, from that very first instant when we met, everything, it all says that you want me as much as I want you.'

He gripped her savagely for a moment, a stark anger on his face. Pagan stiffened with a spasm of fear, but now that the heat of their ardour had been somewhat doused she was able to sit up and push him away.

Face flushed, she told him, 'Maybe that's just you, making grand assumptions. You have such a fine opinion of yourself, you seem to think everybody has to fall for you.'

'You seemed to have a pretty good opinion of me five minutes ago,' he jibed.

She blushed, glad of the dark.

'I won't deny you look good,' she admitted, 'but there's got to be more than just animal lust between people.'

'I've done quite well on what you call animal lust so far,' he told her.

'Maybe that's why you're not married, have no roots, move from one hotel to another, and have to make do with a woman like the one in the next room for company!'

It was a shot in the dark in more senses than one, but she felt him tense beside her.

'That was intended to hurt, wasn't it?' He laughed mirthlessly. 'As they say, if you can't stand the heat, get out of the kitchen.'

Pagan tried to move off the bed, but he put his arms round her waist and pulled her back, winding himself round her with his head buried in the softness of her stomach.

She desperately wanted to run her fingers through the golden strands of his hair, and trying not to disturb him she bent her head for one luxurious instant and let her lips touch his head with a gesture so gentle that he didn't even notice. Hot tears coursed silently down her cheeks once more. How she wanted to lose herself in his embrace, to press her lips, as he had done, against the intimate flesh of his body! Instead she rested one hand on the packed muscle of his shoulder and tried to ease him away.

'Stay with me till morning,' he pleaded. There was an unexpected note of supplication in his voice that sent a shudder of longing through her.

'I want to go home now.' Her voice was small and strained.

'You make me feel like a heel, my darling,' he said at last. 'I honestly thought you were teasing. Tell me something, Pagan, you were unsure, weren't you? You almost gave in?'

'Does it matter?' she asked coldly. 'It's not some sort of competition, is it, where you have to make a girl give in to you just to prove you can do it?'

'I must have you.' It was a flat statement with no emotion in it.

'You sound like some feudal baron! Whatever happened to equality?'

'That's exactly what I'd like to know.' He raised his head. 'Here you are, to all intents and purposes a liberated lady, and it turns out you're still a virgin. Are you telling the truth? I can soon find out.'

'I don't lie!' She was suddenly angry. 'And why liberated should only mean being free to say yes escapes me. I *am* free. And as it happens, I choose to say no. Also,' she added, 'I've spent the last four years since leaving boarding school looking after my seventy-year-old uncle and trying to run a sailing school. It hasn't left much time, or inclination, for anything else. So stop making fun of me as if I'm some sort of freak! I'm not.' Her voice rose of its own accord. 'You don't know what it's been like!' she almost shouted before being able to bring the sudden access of pent up feelings under control.

Unexpectedly Leale kissed her gently on the cheek.

'It's all right, my love, my darling. It's all right—I understand.' He kissed her brow and slid his lips along her damp hairline. 'I know how work can make captives of us and then after a while it seems to be all there is. I know all about that.'

Pagan felt him looking at her in the dark with his face very close but not now touching her own.

'I know all about that.' He sighed. 'How do you think it is for me? I have to be detached in my relationships because there are always other things uppermost in my mind—essential things which can have at stake the livelihoods of many people. And because I never know when I'm going to come back to a place I have to take what I want when I see it. There may be no second chance.' He sat up and tried to cradle her in his arms. 'You don't imagine that I don't realise the sham of my sort of life, do you? But what else can I do? There's no way out. Women fall into two categories— good-time girls looking for the richest pickings, like Michelle, and the clinging type who want children and a man who comes home at the same time every evening. What choice is that?'

'You've got a very limited imagination!' She pushed herself free and stood up beside the bed.

'What do you mean?'

Pagan didn't answer. What was the point?

'What do you mean?' Leale repeated more force-fully.

'I mean your categories are rather limited, aren't they? I mean, *I'm* not like that. I'm not a gold-digger, on the hunt for some man to keep me. I'll fend for myself, thank you very much. Nor do I envisage the boredom of being a harassed housewife, sitting at home waiting for her man. No, thank you to that as well. I've got a life of my own to live.'

'So there!' he mocked.

'You're insufferable!'

Pagan felt humiliated to be standing there without a

stitch on, dark though it was, with only the light coming through from the other room. The thought of this tough, unashamedly virile man lying naked on the bed in front of her, visible only by means of a shaft of light through the half-open door, was novel. With a shock she realised she had never seen a man without his clothes before. Not a man like this, anyway. The boys swimming naked in the lake on hot summer days didn't count.

She couldn't suppress a little giggle.

'What on earth's the matter? Have you been having me on?'

In a trice he was bolt upright beside her, dragging her back to an uncomfortable proximity against his body.

Fighting free, she said innocently, 'I didn't realise men really did look like Greek discus throwers.'

'What?'

'You know, Greek statues.'

She remembered the Michelangelo statues in Florence. Not David, he was too young, but those statues of mature, muscled men, semi-reclining, as Leale was now at this moment.

She felt, rather than saw, his smile flash in the dark.

'You're a ridiculous child,' he told her, 'but you're making me feel as bashful as a girl must feel when some chap makes a personal comment about her physical attributes.' There was an ironic edge to his bantering. 'Does this mean that you're beginning to regard me as a sex object?'

Pagan moved out of his grasp, searching among the clothes on the floor for her panties.

'Or aren't I good enough for you, Pagan?' came the voice softly in the dark. 'Is that it?'

She was taken aback by the unexpectedness of the question and looked at him quickly to see if he was smiling, but his eyes gleamed back at her without a glint of humour and there was a strangely watchful look on his face.

In a sudden flash of intuition she felt she had hit on

something important. His very stillness seemed to add to the serious note they had somehow struck.

She knelt beside the bed. 'You have to go on proving things to yourself all the time, don't you?' she asked softly. 'You have to prove you can make the most money, have the most women, have the best body, drive the fastest car.' She touched the back of his hand. 'Why, Leale? Why?'

He didn't answer.

She felt a kinship with him and was moved by her sudden awareness of the desperation behind his self-confident, bantering exterior.

His voice was defensive when he spoke. 'Why should I be content with third rate? Why should I make do with second best? And what about you? You want to be the fastest woman to sail the Atlantic.'

'I know,' she answered simply. 'But I'm not driven by my ambition. I drive it.'

Leale kept very still for a moment. It seemed like an eternity before he slowly put out a tentative hand towards her and grasped her two hands in his one big one.

'Thank you, Pagan.' He let her hands drop.

She didn't ask what he meant. It was a connection between them that was more powerful than lust and needed no other means of communication.

With a swift movement Leale swung athletically off the bed and started to help her find her clothes. When they were both dressed he held her carefully in his strong arms for a moment.

'I said I'd drive you back to pick up your car. Are you ready?'

'I left my jacket in the other room,' she answered with a look at the adjoining door.

'Wait here.' He came back in a moment with her jacket. 'You may as well forget young Bobby for tonight. Come out this way.'

He tactfully led her out through another door into a dressing-room and from there into a study. In a moment he had unlocked the outer door and they were standing in the dimly lit corridor with its ornate Victorian sconces casting discreet shadows along the silent corridors. Without exchanging more than a word or two they went downstairs and let themselves out through the carved door at the front.

The sky seemed to be full of stars, and a light breeze blew in from the lake. No one saw them arrive and no one had seen them leave. It seemed a very lonely way to live to Pagan. She glanced tenderly at her companion. It was illogical, the confusion of emotion he seemed to arouse inside her.

'You seem to treat this place like your own home,' she remarked as lightly as she could.

A sadness showed itself fleetingly in his face. 'It would be nice, wouldn't it? A family home, instead of a small hotel. Children playing in the gardens——'

She shivered, remembering the image which had flashed through her mind the first time she had come to this place. She told him about it.

He shrugged it away. 'Don't make anything of it. People's lives mesh briefly. It happens that if they're lucky they find themselves on the same wave-length for a time, then,' he clicked his fingers, 'they move on. The link is broken.'

'No,' she countered, appalled at the bleakness of his vision. 'If the connection is strong it never breaks.'

'Try living my kind of life,' he derided, leading the way towards the car. 'You'd soon realise the tenuousness of most relationships. Most people depend on habit to keep them together. Break the habit and they soon find someone else.'

He let her into the car.

'That's a very sad thing to believe,' she murmured. 'I feel that——' she paused. 'When, that is, when I fall in love, it'll be for ever.'

'You ought to be in the song-writing game,' he told her curtly.

She blushed at being put down so abruptly. Then something he had said when they first met came back to her and she said, quoting him, 'I believe what I want to believe.'

Leale gripped the steering-wheel but let the engine idle for a moment or two.

'I hope for your sake you find a man worthy of such fidelity!'

He started to ease the car up the drive between the trees. Only the light from the dashboard illumined the harsh set of his face. It was like a mask he put on whenever there was any danger that she was going to probe too far.

Feeling that she would never get a second chance, that the rare intimacy which seemed to have built between them once the question of sex had been for the moment shelved, that this moment was never to be repeated, she asked, 'Don't you still have some feeling that you're linked with the friends of your schooldays? Why can't a grown-up love between a man and woman be as permanent?'

He laughed harshly and his face seemed to twist into a mask of derision.

'Your schooldays may have been full of friendship; mine were quite different.' He drove swiftly and expertly along the main road towards the town. Then he shot a brief sideways look at her. 'Don't you realise how fortunate people like you are? Growing up in a small community among friends and relations? My childhood was spent moving from school to school, town to town, always one jump ahead of the bailiffs, with a father who was either celebrating his luck at the tables with his own cheap whisky or drowning the memory of his losses with that of other people. I had no childhood.'

'What about your mother?' Pagan asked.

'There was a photograph. I remember the smell of cheap scent. Whether it was her or some other woman, who knows?'

He glanced sardonically down at her. 'Sad, isn't it?'

His glance raked over her, taking in the eyes luminous with sympathy for him.

'Doesn't it make you feel sorry enough——' he asked silkily, 'to want to get in the back of the car with me when I stop?'

Pagan drew sharply back from him. 'It's worked before, has it?' she asked in a tight little voice.

'Countless times,' he purred, his eyes gleaming in the dark.

'If the women you fancied were a little more intelligent, you'd have to refine your technique somewhat,' she told him stiffly.

'It nearly worked with you,' he murmured, 'my love.' He took one hand off the steering wheel long enough to run his fingers down the back of her wrist.

'Nearly is only a might-have-been,' she retorted crisply, falling back on a childhood saying.

'Too true,' he agreed. 'But I still think if I'd pushed I would have been able to take you back there in the hotel. You ought to thank me.'

Pagan was silent. Eventually she said, 'No, I don't think so somehow.'

'That took some thinking about.' Leale glanced down quickly. His eyes searched her face.

She turned away. He was so beautiful, it hurt when he looked at her like that. All she wanted was to be in his arms.

He drove the car into the market square and pulled up behind the Renault with the motorbike still parked next to it. Somehow they looked rather forlorn in the empty expanse of the usually bustling square.

Leale got out and came round to Pagan's side of the car and pulled her to her feet. Then he folded her into his arms.

'Thank you for the compliment of taking so long over the answer to that question of mine.' He kissed her lightly on the forehead. 'It makes it a little easier to accept that you're the one that got away.'

Then he led her to her car and stood silently by while she fumbled in her bag for her keys. There seemed to be things that should be said between them now, before the night ended and the chance was lost for ever. But she could find no way of sorting out the right words and she could only go through the mechanical movements of fitting the key in the lock, opening the car door and settling herself in the driving seat.

'Don't forget your lights,' Leale warned quietly.

With a set face Pagan clicked them on. It was over. He had at least been honest about what he wanted of her. She looked up at him. Her eyes seemed to him huge in the half-light.

'Do you want me to follow part of the way back to make sure you get back all right?' he asked.

'I know how to drive,' she replied, her answer acid with unhappiness.

'You've had more to drink than you probably realise,' he countered. He paused. Then, as if coming to a swift decision, he turned without another word and walked back to his own car.

Miserably Pagan started the engine. It was with a kind of forlorn sense of intimacy that she watched the dipped headlights tracking her all the way back along the twists and turns of the lake road. When she reached the turning into the lane that led to her cottage she half-hoped that despite the inevitable outcome, he would signal for her to stop, but the lights behind dipped once, then he was driving past, gaining speed, driving away from his hotel, away from her and out of her life, along the road that climbed and twisted up into the black desolation of the remotest fells.

'Waterproofs?' Pagan handed a jacket to Ginny's mother.

The rain that had threatened all weekend had finally reached them late on Sunday morning and it swept the foreshore in mean gusts, pitching the dinghies about in unexpected formations, and bringing a raw, red cold to all their faces.

Luckily there was only the afternoon to survive now, and Pagan tried to smile with a cheer she did not feel.

Jan had worked the whole weekend and had positively oozed energy and good humour, while Tim had gone around with a cheese-grin on his face and half an eye on Jan all the time as if he daren't let her out of his sight. Pagan had noticed how quick he had been to take over when, as usual, Jan had put her shoulder to one of the Wayfarers to help push it down to the waterline, and she wondered if, later on, he would start to lay down the law about the things he was going to allow the mother-to-be to do. Of course, they would all take as much of the heavy work from Jan as possible, but too much solicitude on Tim's part might be awkward. There was no knowing at this stage just how the prospect of fatherhood was going to affect him.

The weekend had gone surprisingly well despite the weather. The little Robinson boy had settled down after a stint with Leale and he had spent the morning alone with Ginny and her mother in a mirror dinghy. Pagan thought it was time to let René get used to handling the boat herself now, but it had been a bit of an experiment to put the boy and the girl together.

Ginny came up to have her lifejacket checked. She was sweet, with her little flaxen pigtails and enveloping waterproofs, and she smiled a gap-toothed smile at Pagan.

'I'm going to helm again all by myself,' she told Pagan. 'And so is Terry. I can gybe better than him. But he can tie a sheepshank quicker than me!' She grinned up at Pagan. 'We wanted to ask if you'll tick some things off in our log-books now.' She looked back to where Terry was standing by the water's edge.

'What do you want me to tick off?' asked Pagan, bending down a little so that she was on the same level as the ten-year-old.

'Knots and things, and safety, and capsize drill,' she answered, all in a rush.

'Tell you what,' suggested Pagan, 'we'll have a quick test at the end of the afternoon. It's raining now, so you may feel like coming in a little earlier than usual.'

'Goodee!' piped Ginny. 'I'll go and tell Terry.' She ran off, Minnie-Mouse-like in her red sailing boots.

Terry had evidently been waiting to see what Pagan had to say, for Ginny went straight to him where he was standing on the jetty. His pale face lit up at once when the girl spoke to him and he took Ginny by the arm and ran with her towards the mirror.

Pagan turned to René. 'They're coming on very well, both of them,' she said. 'You all seemed to get on famously this morning.'

'Poor little mite,' said René, pulling a sad mouth. 'He's a bit lost, that one. He needs mothering. He seems to have spent the last few years being pushed from pillar to post.'

Pagan was called away by someone at that point and with a brief invitation for them to bring the boat back in whenever they had had enough, the two women parted. But René's words echoed in her mind with an unexpected and painful resonance. How many adults, now regarded as in their prime, were at heart nothing but lost boys? She grimaced. She knew at least one. Sympathy, however, seemed misplaced when she recalled his image to mind. The arrogant and successful businessman he undoubtedly was mocked her tenderer feelings.

A brief glance towards the trees that waved on the edge of the garden beyond the lane revealed the deeply pitched roof of the Manor House, one of the upstairs rooms between the white-painted gables, visible, its dark oblong of window unblinking in the steadily thickening drizzle. Pagan tore her eyes away and made for the jetty.

Bobby, seemingly oblivious to the rain and wearing

shorts with only a waterproof shell under his lifejacket, was fixing the pump up to bail out one of the Wayfarers. He hadn't exactly avoided Pagan all weekend, but it had seemed that there was always someone else around whenever they needed to speak to each other.

Pagan had been surprised to see him at all on Saturday morning and she had taken the precaution of asking another student along as a stopgap should her companion of Friday night fail to show up. Bobby, misunderstanding, had seemed to take this as an implied threat to his job, and he had worked flat out all weekend with none of his usual fooling about.

As she came up behind him Pagan wondered whether she should say anything to let him off the hook. He was a good worker anyway and she didn't want him to think she harboured any secret recriminations against him for the way he had behaved at the hotel.

His muscular back was bent over the pump and he didn't hear her soft tread in rubber boots until she was standing right behind him on the wooden jetty.

'Hey!' she called down to him. He raised his head from his task and she jumped down into the boat beside him. His eyes were apprehensive at first. She cuffed him on the arm, 'What about giving a run-down on racing tactics to those two bigger lads this afternoon?' she asked. 'They've only got one more weekend of their block of lessons to go, and you're about as well qualified as anybody.'

He grinned. 'Hey, do you mean it, Pagan? That'd be great! If I have to go slowly once round the bay again I'll go bonkers!'

He unhooked the nozzle of the pump and started to junk it all back on the jetty. Then he bit his lip rather bashfully before saying, 'I didn't know whether I was in your bad books or not.'

Pagan took heart from his discomfiture. Somehow she began to feel very old and very wise. It was a new feeling, and not without a trace of sadness in it. She felt she would never know what it was to be really young, free to be gloriously foolish instead of merely awkwardly inept and naïve whenever she was caught out of her depth.

'I hope everything worked out to your satisfaction,' she told him cheekily.

Bobby's responsive chuckle was worth the effort it cost her to be flippant. But didn't she just have to keep things running smoothly?

This must be maturity, she told herself as she walked back up the shingle with the pump. All she wanted to do was hide away somewhere and cry until her store of tears was drained.

Tim and Jan were keen to come and inspect the racing yacht that had been mentioned as a contest possibility by Wilson. After Pagan's description of her encounter with the Promotions Manager, his name had developed into a joke among them, so that when Tim, later that afternoon, had called across from the safety launch as Pagan sailed past with four pupils aboard a GP12, he had said, 'I've got Tuesday afternoon off. Is that O.K. for Mr Wilson?' she knew exactly what he meant.

'I rang the boatyard yesterday,' she called, indicating to the man at the helm to bring the G.P. head to wind for a moment. 'They said any time at all would do, so we could drive out there after lunch if you like.'

He gave her a thumbs-up sign and started up the motor again. He would continue his vigil in the middle of the bay until all the novices were safely back to land.

'They must imagine we're loaded even to be considering looking at a boat like this,' Pagan mused when, on the Tuesday following they rattled along in the Renault towards the coast. 'What do you imagine they'll do when we turn up at the gates in this old bone-shaker?'

'They'll try to sell us the nearest rubber dinghy, I expect,' Jan grinned.

But their reception by the man who was in charge of the boatyard, a Mr Holton, was nothing if not cordial.

He led them through into a large wooden building almost as spacious as an aircraft hangar where boats of all shapes and sizes and in various stages of construction were being worked on.

The noise was deafening from a power saw and the man had to shout to make himself heard. He pointed down the shed towards the far end where it opened out towards the slipway and the gleaming hulk of a very sleek-looking racing yacht met their gaze.

Pagan's eyes rounded and she turned to him. He nodded and mouthed something in the uproar. Pagan felt her fingers begin to tingle with excitement.

'There she is!' announced the man in the sudden silence as the saw was switched off.

There was a pride in his voice which found a matching response now in Pagan's thoughts. It was as if her imagination had been set on fire, and the weight of hopeless longing for the man she couldn't have was lifted for a while as she turned to the manager to ply him with countless questions as to the boat's specifications. Tim and Jan clustered round, interested too, but their enthusiasm could not match the greed with which Pagan lapped up the man's words.

Her eyes were dark when the question of finance cropped up. Briefly she explained the situation to him. When Wilson's firm was mentioned his own face clouded momentarily and he told her quietly, after a brief look over his shoulder, to tread carefully where they were concerned.

'I'll tell you something confidential, like,' he said, taking her to one side. 'It's all due to a back word from one of their directors that we've got this little lady on our hands now. It was ordered some time ago, but work had to stop six weeks since when he couldn't bring the account up to date.' He tapped his lips. 'I'm telling you that, because if you want to make an offer, it might be a useful thing to know. . . .' He gave her a wink.

'I still don't see how I'm going to be able to make any sort of offer yet,' Pagan told him wistfully, 'but thanks for the tip. At least you know I'm interested, and if you get an offer for her before I can come up with anything, I hope you'll keep me informed.'

'Will do,' agreed the man. 'She'll handle nicely, even by a girl, and when the self-steering is rigged up it'll be a doddle.' He beckoned to a workman who was passing, 'Let's have a look at them plans for *Silver Lady*,' he called. 'Come on up, love.'

He led Pagan up some wooden steps in a corner of the hangar to the place where he had his office. Through the glass windows which ran the length of it she could see down into the hangar. *Silver Lady* gleamed dully in its undercoat of matt preservative at the far end. Pagan felt that there was only one thing in her life she had ever wanted as much as she wanted such a yacht.

Jan and Tim were standing beneath the supporting struts looking up at the sleek hull. Their admiration was evident in their every gesture.

When Pagan had pored over the plans and read the specifications as carefully as any love letter and when they had all been offered hot mugs of tea as if to seal some sort of agreement, they had tumbled out of the boatyard wreathed in grins.

There was the tang of the open sea in the air, for the yard was situated on the estuary only a mile from the mouth of the river and it seemed to add a wild air of intoxication to their mood.

'I *must* have it. I *must*!' cried Pagan, throwing her arms up in an uncharacteristic gesture of exhilaration. 'It's the most beautiful yacht I've ever seen. What do you think, Tim? Really, without pulling any punches?'

'It seems perfect,' he told her simply.

'Too perfect,' the practical voice of Jan broke in. 'It costs a hell of a lot, Pagan. There's a recession on. What sort of company is in a position to spend money on a yacht, for goodness' sake? You're really going to have to work hard to coax that sort of money from anyone.'

Sobered by the realisation that what Jan said was true, they made their way back towards the car.

'If some company would buy it and let me give them all the publicity by sailing it, and winning that damned race, everything would be roses. But it's if, if, if!' sighed Pagan.

'It's the problem of finding a company able to make that sort of investment in the present economic climate, as Jan says,' judged Tim.

'Especially round here,' added Jan. 'Perhaps you ought to look further afield, Pagan? Manchester or somewhere like that?'

'Yes, it's big money you have to find, Pagan, if you're really serious about all this, because it's not just the ship, it's fitting out with all the latest racing aids, it's provisions, it's medical supplies, it's——'

'Please!' cried Pagan, stopping her ears with her hands. 'Don't you think I've kept myself awake at nights going over and over all the possibilities? I've been driving myself mad with the problem. But still I haven't found a proper solution. I know it's a lot of money, but the only thing to do is to keep on writing letters and talking to people. Someone somewhere must say yes before long.'

'But how long can you keep on doing that?' asked Tim, not trying to depress her any further, his kind brown eyes showing only concern for her.

'I'll go on till I succeed,' she averred.

She leant against the car for a moment. A sea wind had got up and it lifted the loose fronds of her chestnut hair, teasing it back from her face so that her expression was revealed in all its fierce determination.

'If I miss this year's race, I'll try again in two years' time when they hold the next one.'

Tim and Jan looked at her with almost parental concern.

'Two years is a long time at your age,' said Jan at last. 'Perhaps other things will seem more important by then,' she smiled, relaxing.

Pagan turned bright eyes on her. 'If you mean marriage, you can count me out. Two years, ten years, it'll make no difference. This is what I've got to do and this is what I'll do, come hell or high water!'

She looked across the car roof at the couple. They were nice people, but a gulf separated them. Sometimes she felt as if she was from a different planet. Jan thought she was a dreamer and no matter how hard she tried to explain, neither of them would ever really understand the fever in her blood. Only Uncle Henry had understood that—the wanderlust. But he was gone.

A chill wind seemed to blow through her. It was true what she had just told them. Two years, ten years, she would do it. And, she knew, she would have to do it alone.

Undaunted, she grinned back at them.

'Don't look so worried,' she laughed. 'I'm not crackers—just ambitious. I'm going to solve this problem the way Uncle Henry used to solve all his problems.' She chuckled at the expectant look in their faces. 'Tonight,' she told them, 'I'm going to sleep on it.'

The talk was desultory on the way back as if nobody really wanted to go over the problems facing Pagan again, but were unable to find anything else to grip their attention either. Even the topic of the new baby seemed to have taken second place for a while.

It was only when Pagan was driving back to the boathouse for a bite to eat after their excursion that Jan spoke up. They were slowing down by the gates of the old Manor House ready to make the turn into the home lane when she caught sight of the big white convertible displayed bang in the middle of the crescent-shaped gravel drive in front of the house.

'There's your man,' she announced. 'By all accounts he wouldn't even notice the purchase of a yacht like that. It'd be nothing but a small addendum to his weekly shopping list.'

Pagan hung on to the steering wheel and swung the car too fast into the lane.

'Steady on!' warned Tim, putting a protective arm round Jan.

Pagan's face was set grimly as she brought the car to a jolting stop. She turned to Jan as she got out. 'Any more bright ideas like that?' she asked flippantly as she swung the keys in her hand.

Jan grinned, 'That's the best so far!'

'Keep thinking,' riposted Pagan as she led the way to the house. 'Just keep thinking!'

CHAPTER EIGHT

THAT night as Pagan snuggled under her duvet she was as good as her word and repeated the childish formula which Uncle Henry had always avowed was the sure solution to any knotty problem. Someone had once explained it to her with the theory that, the mind being a far more complex bit of machinery than any one of us really appreciated, if we slotted a problem into it and left it to get on with doing its job, sooner or later an answer was bound to pop out. A bit like a slot machine at a fair, thought Pagan cynically. But she was desperate enough to try any crazy scheme, the price of postage stamps and her enthusiasm for pounding out begging letters on her portable having both their different limits.

'You know the answer really,' she told her brain sternly as she drifted off to sleep, 'so just do your stuff!'

It was with a sense of disappointment that she woke next morning to find no magic solution to the problem.

She had had the deepest most dreamless sleep for a long time. 'At least I've hit on a cure for insomnia,' she thought, then she shivered. It hadn't been entirely dreamless. In one of those fleeting images which often come on the verge of waking up and are usually impossible to recall when fully awake, she had seen a face. At least, she had sensed a face. Slowly she forced it back into her mind.

She had been trying to pull one of the little dinghies up on to the beach. Yet the harder she pulled, the heavier it seemed to become. Sweat had begun to pour down her arms and eventually in the dream Pagan had managed to turn round to see what was pulling the boat back into the lake. She had been mortified to see Leale de Laszlo, impeccably dressed in something dark and expensive-looking, wearing an unaccustomed white shirt, its cuffs dazzling in the gloom—almost as dazzling as the gleam of his teeth as he drew his lips back in a sardonic smile. He was standing nonchalantly by the water's edge, the water lapping, but not wetting, his black leather shoes.

What her eyes really focussed on, though, was his hand, where she could see in sharp detail how he was holding on to the transom of the dinghy. She knew, in the dream, that he only had to raise his hand to release it and she would be able to bring the boat easily into shore.

Cross with herself for letting him penetrate even her dreams, she lay in bed for a full ten minutes. To be sensible she ought to give some objective, rational thought to the dream. That had been the point of the exercise. But her waking thoughts were shy and sensitive to the pain of approaching the subject of Leale too closely.

'It's all nonsense anyway,' she told herself, dragging slowly out of bed.

The next few weeks progressed uneventfully enough. Pagan's appetite seemed to be almost non-existent these days, and she found she was rarely sleeping a whole night through. She became obsessed with work and now seldom went for a drink with the rest of the crowd after lessons were over, preferring, it seemed, to go back to the cottage alone to swot up on her other 'work', the big race.

Jan noticed the change in her manner and tried to jolly her out of it, but Pagan would allow herself only a grim smile before carrying on as before. Less and less did she bother to change out of her sailing gear when she got in at night, and she stopped wearing make-up altogether. The first weeks of June were scorchingly hot so that, despite her thinner, haunted look, her skin began to glow a golden brown, giving her a gamine, waif-like appearance.

She couldn't fail to be conscious of the extensive rebuilding going on at the Manor. Every day contractors' lorries stood in the front drive or round at the back and there was always the sound of men working.

After the first few days Leale's car had failed to appear outside the house and she guessed he had gone away. This was confirmed a week or so later when, meeting her old school-friend by chance in town, she learned that he and most of the staff brought up from the main office in London had vacated the first suite, reserving only a small suite of rooms on the third floor for Leale's personal use.

'It's interesting, being a telephonist at a hotel like ours,' Anne confided. 'It's more like a family than a hotel.'

Pagan couldn't bring herself to ask when Leale would be returning, but she didn't need to ask. Anne was a mine of unsolicited information.

'Mr de Laszlo's away in New York for the next six weeks. He and his girlfriend, that Michelle, are having the Manor restored exactly as it used to be. It looks as if he's planning to live in it permanently. Imagine, a place that size! He was out buying antiques before he left and she's been waltzing in and out with wallpaper and fabric samples all week. Nothing ever seems to be good enough for her——'

'Didn't she leave with him?' Pagan's curiosity was aroused.

'No, and don't we know it!'

'So she's staying there alone, is she?' Pagan mused, half to herself.

'Alone? You must be joking!' Anne's expression told her what nature of company the blonde was keeping.

'He's as bad, I expect,' shrugged Pagan.

But Anne just pursed her mouth noncommittally. 'I don't know about that,' she said after a pause. 'He seems to work all hours. A proper workaholic he is. Very nice, though—a real gentleman and very quiet.'

'Quiet?' Pagan looked incredulous, but Anne was already moving off.

'That's my bus there,' she said. 'See you around, Pagan. Say hello to Faynia for me!'

With that she was gone, and Pagan walked off down the street with a small frown puckering her brow.

There was no time in the days ahead to allow her thoughts to dwell on anything but work, however. They were entering what she had jokingly referred to as the vicious stage of the season and bookings were coming in now for mid-week lessons too.

Usually she liked this part of the year best, for despite the long hours, the weather was usually excellent and as it was still in the school term most of the pupils were adults, so that it was fascinating to meet so many different types.

This season, though, she had no heart for it. She became fed up too with the men who inevitably thought it in order to flirt with her, persistent in their invitations to dinner and lakeside drives. It was as if her humiliation over Leale had wounded her so deeply that she couldn't yet trust herself even to casual dating. No one could measure up to Leale, so what was the point?

'It's not that I'm a prude,' she confided to Faynia on a rare day off, 'and I don't think I'm frigid. It's just that it doesn't seem right, to be so casual about a thing like that. And anyway, what's the point of going out to dinner with them anyway. They're not going to get what they want, and I'm just going to be bored out of my mind for an evening. I'd rather stay at home with a good book.'

'Perhaps you just don't fancy any of your current suitors?' replied Faynia sagely. 'I shouldn't let it worry you.'

'I don't think I'm ever going to fancy anyone ever again——'

'Again?' Faynia raised her eyebrows.

The slip was enough to make Pagan colour violently.

'You're not still pining for King Rat, are you?' demanded Faynia in astonishment.

Pagan felt as if she was suddenly looking through a wall of tears.

'Love,' soothed Faynia, patting her on the shoulder. 'It's hell, I know. But it'll wear off, give it time.'

Pagan shook her head, unable to speak. 'It won't,' she managed to gulp at last. 'I'll love him for ever.'

Faynia didn't say anything. She went through into the shop and when she came back Pagan was pale-faced but dry-eyed once again and getting ready to leave.

'It's the Hunt Ball next week,' she told Pagan. 'You need something to put on a good dress for. Why not let me ask John to get a couple of tickets for you? You could bring that sailor boy of yours. He seems good fun.'

Pagan tried a wan smile. 'Bobby, you mean?'

She and Bobby, despite what had happened, still met at Renoir's once a week, but always in a crowd, and it was always the last minute until Pagan thought she supposed she ought to go out one night a week. They had neither of them mentioned Michelle since that weekend.

'I'm really busy right now. Perhaps next year.' She tried to smile. Next year? It seemed impossible to think so far ahead. Everything would be different then. Leale would be no more than a painful memory.

Faynia didn't press the invitation to the Ball. Nor did she make any secret of the fact that she regarded it as a feather in her cap to have persuaded John to take her.

'Absolutely everybody will be there. It's the event of the season!'

Pagan sighed. Her season was composed of quite different events. In a few weeks the entries for the yacht race would have to be submitted, and so far she was no nearer to a solution than before.

Downhearted, she left Faynia, and on the drive back to the cottage she did some serious thinking. It seemed to be her habitual occupation these days in the odd moments of solitude that came her way, and a familiar theme was beginning to emerge.

Try as she would she could not avoid the way her thoughts came continually back to Leale de Laszlo. It seemed as if he was the key to the whole problem.

She went through the litany again.

Was it true she'd found the perfect racing craft?—Yes, came the answer. Was it true that she needed a benefactor rich enough to finance the said craft?—Yes, again, came the answer. And was it true that in all the people she had come across only Leale de Laszlo could afford the considerable investment necessary for the whole project?—inevitably the answer came, yes.

In a foul temper she stamped into the house.

It was too much like the time she had had to go to him, cap in hand, over the right of way. The only difference this time was that she knew to the smallest detail exactly what manner of man she was dealing with. She could imagine the devilish gleam in those sometimes cold, sometimes brightly sea-coloured eyes, as he listened to her request.

'I won't do it—I can't!' she told herself, as she slammed about the kitchen.

She couldn't settle to anything. The cottage seemed like a prison. It was her own thoughts, however, which made the prison, holding her confined within them until she could summon the strength to break out.

Unable to bear being indoors any longer, she stamped outside. The day was sultry, typical of mid-June in this part of the country. The lake lay like a block of molten blue metal within the sharply etched confines of the mountains which surrounded it.

Unable to bear the heat, Pagan had put on a cotton sun-dress for the first time this year, and it set off the light tan she had inevitably acquired from her days

outdoors. Slimmer now, with no make-up and her hair
floating loosely around her shoulders, her face was
hauntingly beautiful, and she seemed to have acquired a
new fragility which softened the tomboyish look of old.

She began to make her way to the top of the lane
leading down to the foreshore. It seemed aeons ago
since she had skidded to an astonished halt at the sight
of the 'Keep Out' sign outside the Manor, and she
couldn't help looking through the trees to where the
contractors' vans were still parked. Electricity, gas,
central heating, and now painters and decorators were
there. The house, half painted outside, with scaffolding
still adorning the west wing, was beginning to regain
some of its former splendour.

Soon, she thought, the white car would be back
again, and it would become a regular feature, if Anne
was to be believed and Leale really intended to use the
place as a home.

Somehow Pagan couldn't quite imagine it. Not if it
meant that Michelle would be set up in it, mistress of
the Manor, to rule the roost while Leale was away on
business. The old place would see some unaccustomed
goings-on if that were to be the case. The graciousness
of former days which was being so carefully restored
would be lost for ever.

The lake, when she reached the shore, was like glass.
Not a breath of air ruffled its surface. The fells were
reflected perfectly in reverse in it, even the colours were
faithful reproductions in a natural looking-glass. It was
a day very different from the one on which she had first
caught sight of the red, white and blue sail of Leale's
windboard. Anyone would be hard put to move across
the surface of this motionless expanse, light airs sailor
or no.

Pagan remembered his correction when, in her
innocence, she had called him that. There had been no
mistaking his meaning when he had claimed he liked a
challenge so long as the prize was worth it. But it gave

her only pain and no satisfaction at all to realise that she was one prize for which the challenger had had to concede defeat.

Still restless, she debated whether to take one of the boats out, but it hardly seemed worth it, in the stillness of such a day. Instead she walked along the shore towards the garden of the Manor, to the place where it met the shoreline and a mellow brick wall marked the boundary of the two properties. As a child she had often clambered over the wall and walked up to the house over the well-kept lawns. Curious to see whether work had started on the gardens yet, she scrambled up the wall and crouched there on top in order to survey the secret places of long ago.

Flowers spread in wild abandon before her eyes. Like a child, and with a little smile of melancholy pleasure, she dropped lightly down on to the other side. The earth was soft underfoot where, it was obvious, no one had walked for some time. The roses which had been the pride and joy of the Colonel were overgrown now, bushes rising up in straggling disarray, the trellis roses fallen, long shoots stretching with wild grace over the moss-covered path. Colours rioted before her eyes and the air was heady with the rich perfume of roses coming into full bloom.

She had only gone a pace, revelling in the unexpected rediscovery of such a secret place, when a voice seemed to come at her from the sky. She looked up with a disbelieving shudder of recognition. Just in time she caught a glimpse of the long form of Leale de Laszlo reclining nonchalantly along the solid curved branch of the giant oak, before he came swinging down to a branch above her head. She had been so busy picking her way amongst the trails of roses that she had failed to notice his jacket lying on the ground beneath the tree, and now he looked laconically down at her from his vantage point.

To say she was covered in confusion would be an

understatement. She felt first hot, then cold sweep over her body. For a moment her fists tightened by her sides and words fled.

He looked leaner, tougher, not quite so healthily tanned as before, but his hair still gleamed, outrageously blond, still too long, and his eyes, sparking bright waves in sunlight, still held that dangerous half bantering, half quizzical look that brought back a flood of unwanted memories.

For what seemed like an eternity they gazed at each other without speaking. Pagan was transfixed by his eyes which pierced her with a laser-like intensity, raking her body from head to foot as if to convince himself that she was made of flesh and blood. She happened to be standing in a patch of sunlight, her hair fine and flyaway, like a halo round her head, her eyes, green and vulnerable, gazing back at him, and, revealed by the white cotton sundress, her neck and shoulders washed to a colour like pale gold.

'I thought it was a flower fairy.' Lazily he uncoiled his muscular frame from its position in the tree and, blue eyes mocking, lively, never leaving her face, he swung his long legs down to the ground.

She was still frozen in one place and watched, gathering her strength to flee should he approach, but he remained by the tree, one hand looped round the branch above his head, the other casually fastened in the broad leather belt of his slick washed denims.

He was wearing a crisp white T-shirt which was taut across his chest and from the short sleeves of which bulged tanned well-shaped arms covered in a down of bright fair hair.

Pagan's glance took in the details without being aware of how she registered them.

'Lost your tongue?' He smiled back at her, equally laconic.

There was another long pause.

Pagan pushed a tangle of chestnut hair from her eyes

and stood motionless in the long grass, unable to answer. It seemed as if all her nerves were tightly tuned ready to send her fleeing back along the overgrown path into the safety of the thicket by the wall.

But, still watching her, Leale remained where he was, holding himself against the oak tree.

At last, jibingly, throwing back at her her own very first words to him, he warned, 'Don't you know you're trespassing?'

She brought herself to frame some words, any words, but they sounded strange to her ears. 'I didn't think anyone would know. It's all so neglected now. . . .' She broke the hold of his glance and looked helplessly around her.

'Did you used to come here in the Colonel's days?' he asked quietly.

Pagan looked fleetingly back at him and nodded.

There came the distant sound of a chaffinch in the wood and for a moment it seemed as if the world stood still and they were both locked in some timeless never-never land.

He was still in shadow, but as she watched, he began to move towards her into the patch of sunlight.

'Don't, I——' She backed off, confusion overwhelming her, then with a superhuman effort, she gathered all her strength. It was now clear beyond a shadow of a doubt what she had to do. Like a gambler betting everything on one last throw of the dice, she squared her shoulders and said, as coolly as she knew how, 'It's a stroke of luck finding you here. I didn't realise you were back yet. I have a business proposition to put to you. I'd be enormously grateful if I could make an appointment to see you to discuss it some time.'

Leale stopped in his advance and a smile played across the lean contours of his face. 'A business proposition? That sounds intriguing!'

He passed a hand over his brow and paused as if waiting for her to go on.

She managed a cool smile, briefly wondering if he knew how much of her composure was an act. 'When would it be convenient?' she asked.

'It's convenient right now,' he told her lazily, his eyes mocking her.

'I'm serious,' she warned him. She gave a deprecating look at the ruined garden in which they stood.

'You'd like somewhere more appropriate?' He seemed to swallow a smile.

It made Pagan regard him icily for a moment and it was on the tip of her tongue to make some excuse to escape when he covered the intervening space between them in two swift strides and took hold of her by the elbow before she could avoid his grasp.

'Come to the house. We'll talk there.'

She had to endure the nearness of his lithe virility and the inescapable pressure of his hand on her arm all the way up the garden. Only when they reached the terrace did he release her.

The ground-floor shutters, she noticed, were still across, but the garden door which led into the rear entrance hall stood open. Painters were busy round the side of the house, but inside it was quiet and empty. Nothing, she observed, had been done so far about interior decoration. In fact the place looked rather neglected as if all interest in it had been lost. She glanced at Leale in surprise.

'All right,' he chided, misunderstanding, 'I'm sorry it's so chaotic. But I *am* treating you seriously. Even if I had to deal with a business *man* he'd have to meet me here in all this mess, as I've moved my office here now.'

He led her through into a small ante-room just off the main hall. It was one room which had been refurbished, yet it was more like a study than an office, with a desk and bookshelves and a phone and not much more.

Pagan noticed a half open suitcase on the floor in the corner with a masculine-looking sponge bag and a razor in a black leather case resting on the top of it. There was also a fluffy-looking brown towel hanging to dry on the radiator.

Quickly Leale folded it up and put it inside the case. 'It's a mess,' he repeated. 'I only got in late last night.'

'Have you left the hotel?' she asked.

He nodded.

'But nothing's finished here!' she exclaimed.

He gave a short laugh. 'Entirely my fault. I called a halt until I'd had a chance to rethink things . . .' he paused. 'I found I wasn't too keen on the choice of interior décor. When it came down to it I realised it was a little too florid for my taste.'

'I wouldn't have thought it mattered, as you won't be here often enough to notice the wallpaper,' she replied tartly.

'It wasn't only the wallpaper I had in mind,' he replied cryptically. 'As I intend to live here more or less permanently, it's important to get it right.'

'Live here?' she gulped.

'I like the peace and quiet. I like this house and——' he stopped abruptly. His face wore a strange expression when he added casually, 'I like lots of things about this particular place, surprisingly enough.'

He leaned against the side of his desk. It seemed to Pagan that his presence filled the room with his sheer physical power and she felt she would easily succumb to his magnetism if she didn't make some effort to ward it off by maintaining an icy distance between them.

Her thoughts started to race. If he said yes to what she was going to ask of him there would be no question of distance between them. Of that she was certain. At least, she mentally corrected herself, so far as physical distance was concerned. It was going to be up to her to maintain unaided any self-preserving inner distance. If she hoped to survive this encounter, she would have to bring every shred of emotional detachment she could muster to their subsequent meetings.

Leale was waiting now to hear what she had to say, so that it was with a feeling as irrevocable as plunging over a cliff edge that she started to tell him about *Silver Lady* and the need for sponsorship.

'Don't tell me about the Race,' he cut in. 'Tell me if you've managed to interest anyone else, or are you asking me to finance the whole shooting match?'

With a lift of her head she told him, 'I've had offers from a food firm to provide provisions, and an electronics firm want me to test some new radio equipment. Other local firms have guaranteed smallish sums so that practically everything can be covered one way or another. The only exception, of course, is the——' she hesitated.

'The yacht itself?' he supplied briskly, with no visible change of expression.

She raised her head and her jaw was set as if to hide from him the weeks of defeat.

'I'd like to see this boat,' he told her. 'When can we go out to have a look at her?'

'Whenever you like,' she answered.

'Come along, then,' he ordered briskly, reaching for his jacket.

Disconcerted by the speed of his response, Pagan could only nod dumbly.

'This doesn't mean I'm saying yes or even maybe,' he warned. 'I just want to see the tub you propose to sail.'

He swung down off the edge of the desk. 'By the way, what do I get out of it, apart from the dubious glory of being associated with a celebrity if you make it across and a tragic heroine if you don't?'

Pagan shivered involuntarily. 'I will make it,' she told him quietly with a lift of her chin. But that wasn't why she had felt the shiver go through her. She had hoped to stall on the question of his cut. She regarded him levelly.

'*Silver Lady* will have a change of name, of course,' she told him. 'Most sponsoring firms like to have the

competing yachts sailing under the company's name.'
She avoided his eyes.

'I rather like *Silver Lady*,' he butted in with a
sidelong grin.

'Well, of course, that's up to you,' she replied coolly.
'But it'll have your company's logo on the sails and
you'll have, as you say, all the publicity from the media,
news, magazine profiles, television and so on. As a
woman competing in a thing like this, and the way
things are,' she added tartly, 'I shall be able to get a lot
of interest—as much as any of the competitors,
perhaps, and much more than if I was a man.'

'As a woman,' he repeated sardonically.

She coloured.

'Are you a woman now?' he provoked.

Her eyes flashed and she drew herself up, but
before she could think of a suitable retort he put two
fingers warningly on her lips and whispered, 'Stormy
weather already?' Her jaw tightened. 'It's all right,' he
was laughing. 'I'm happy to steer clear of squalls at
present!'

He pushed her towards the door. 'Given your evident
distaste for me, it must have cost you something to
come with the begging bowl. Or was it just a spur-of-
the-moment decision when you saw me in the garden?'

Confused, Pagan just looked at him. He smiled
enigmatically. With an effort she pulled herself together
and snapped, 'I'm more businesslike than you give me
credit for! Personal likes and dislikes have nothing to
do with it. I decided last week that I'd approach you on
your return. Nothing can be spur-of-the-moment in this
game.'

Leale nodded briefly. 'Just so long as you realise
you've got to approach it professionally. It won't be a
joy-ride.'

'I'm quite aware of that,' she retorted. She nearly
made some crack about men being all the same—none
of them were capable of taking a woman seriously, but

she thought better of it and merely gritted her teeth as he ushered her outside.

His car had been parked inside the vast garage at the far side of the house. That was how she had missed any warning of his return. Its high-powered luxury seemed to make them airborne and they were at the boatyard in no time. It had been a strangely uncomfortable journey, though short, for Leale, after asking one or two technical questions about *Silver Lady*, had seemed to be able to find nothing else to say to her. He had flicked on the stereo, and after a few moments' unease when she had watched him warily like a cat, she had finally allowed herself to drop her guard and settle back in the deep velour of the upholstery and let the music waft over her.

When the car at last slid to a halt she had her door open before he could come round to do it for her, and with only a brief backward glance to make sure he was following, she strode on ahead into the workshop without another word.

Mr Holton saw her at once from his vantage point in his office up in the roof, and she waved one hand in greeting. He came down at once, obviously pleased, and Pagan turned to introduce him to Leale.

'De Laszlo?' he looked up with a puzzled smile. 'Might that be the firm of de Laszlo International?' he queried. Leale nodded. 'Pleased to do business with you, sir,' said Mr Holton at once, putting out his hand in a warm handshake.

He turned to Pagan with a new look of respect in his eyes. 'If you're going to start anywhere, you may as well start at the top,' he said cryptically.

From then on there was a marked difference in his manner. Whereas before he had merely shown an old-world paternalism towards Pagan, now he was deferential to the point of reverence. Pagan could only watch in growing puzzlement.

When Leale had made a thorough inspection of the

yacht and, refusing a drink on the grounds that he had urgent business waiting for him, had taken her back to the car, she turned to him, tight-lipped.

'So what was all that about?' she demanded. 'If you'd announced yourself as the Emperor of China it couldn't have had a more electrifying effect on the man! What's so special about the name de Laszlo?'

Leale grinned, himself mystified by her reaction. 'You mean you still don't know?' he asked.

Pagan shook her head. 'But I'm dying to be let in on the secret,' she answered caustically.

'I thought you were being clever,' his eyes glittered.

'Perhaps I am without knowing it,' she answered tartly. 'So what's the big secret?'

He shrugged deprecatingly as if almost embarrassed. 'Don't you read the yachting magazines? No——' he paused, 'not the financial sections. I don't suppose you read those.'

'Not much point without any finance, is there?' she glowered.

'If you did do, you'd know I'm a yacht broker.'

'A *what*?' she almost screeched at him. 'Why on earth didn't you tell me?'

'I assumed you knew.'

'Of course I didn't know!' she glowered again, keeping her emotions under control only with an enormous effort. 'How could I know?' What a fool I am, she thought, half turning so that he could not see the flood of humiliating red colouring her face. 'Why should I know a thing like that?' she swung back at him. 'Even if I'd remembered the name I wouldn't necessarily have connected it with you, would I? It would be the natural thing,' she went on sarcastically, 'to expect a firm like that to be run by a short, fat, balding businessman. Not——' she floundered.

'Not what?' he asked with interest.

'Not you!' she snarled.

'I thought you would know,' he repeated, his face

frozen in its expression by the strength of her contempt. 'Why else would you come and ask me to sponsor you?'

'Why come to you?' she mocked. 'A two-year-old would know the answer to that one! You just happen to be the only businessman around here who could afford the expense. And,' she added, 'you seem to have such a lot of moeny to splash around, I don't see why some of it shouldn't come my way.'

Leale regarded her without speaking for a moment. His face had a shuttered look and he gave an almost inaudible sigh as if something had disappointed him beyond words.

'Well, I don't splash my money around for fun. I've seen the yacht; I like her—she seems a good little craft. I'm willing to buy your whole package. Wait——' he held up his hand to forestall her reply. 'Don't thank me yet. You haven't heard my side of it. As I said, I don't splash my money around for fun. There are conditions.'

Pagan raised her head.

He paused.

'Yes?' she urged, holding her breath.

'First, I want it fitted out to my own specifications —Don't worry,' he went on when she opened her mouth to speak, 'I'll stand the cost. There's a lot of excellent new safety equipment on the market. I reserve the right to say what you carry on board.'

'O.K.,' she replied, eyeing him warily. 'And——?'

He had the grace to avoid her eyes and instead turned his head to let his glance drift outside to the breakwater that bounded the car park.

'It's a rather more——' he hesitated, 'a more intimate condition.' He turned to watch her reaction.

Pagan was holding herself rigid with the effort at self-control. So her worst fears were to be confirmed. 'Yes,' she said coolly looking him straight in the eye, 'I think I know what you mean. When would you like to collect?'

There was a sudden stillness in him for a moment. Eyeing her thoughtfully, he said at last as if having consulted a mental time-table, 'We'd better not say after the Race, or you'll be tempted not to come back. What do you think to sometime after contracts have been signed, say the eve of her first sea trials? What you might call,' he added sardonically, 'her maiden voyage?' He raised one eyebrow.

Pagan could have hit him and inside she was a blazing inferno of pure rage, but instead of showing it she lifted her chin and her face was schooled into a mask of total indifference. 'How appropriate,' she replied crisply.

His eyes danced over her. 'Should we shake hands on it? It's the customry way in which to seal a gentleman's agreement.'

'There are no gentlemen present,' she retorted. But without a flicker of visible emotion she drily proffered her right hand.

Leale used it as an excuse to pull her closer to him. His face was only an inch away from her own so that she could feel his warm breath on her cheek when he whispered, 'And perhaps the firm can have something on account now?'

Before she could draw back his lips had found hers, and his kiss was so deep and powerfully slow that she almost found herself responding with treacherous ardour before she managed to check herself and go limp.

He drew back at once when he realised she was unresponsive, and his expression was similarly noncommittal when he murmured, 'Nothing on account? Fair enough.'

Without another word he slipped the car into first gear and they moved off.

CHAPTER NINE

IT was a minor celebration that night in the little timbered pub across the road from the sailing school.

After driving her back from the boatyard, Leale had dropped her at the end of the lane to walk the hundred yards or so to her cottage, and the first thing she did was to ring Tim and Jan to tell them the good news. What the pay-off was going to be, of course, Pagan breathed no word, and she let Tim rattle on innocently about the publicity kickback for Leale's company.

Rather than sit moping alone, licking over her wounds and inevitably questioning whether she was paying too high a price to satisfy her ambition, she rang round several other people who would be interested in the news. Together they had assembled for a celebratory drink, and there were premature good wishes of 'bon voyage' as it got near closing time.

There was only one absentee, and it brought a bitter smile to Pagan's face when she imagined him, doing whatever he was doing in the big house opposite. The ground floor windows were still shuttered, she noticed, and but for the big white convertible that was once again outside in the drive where he must have left it that afternoon there was no sign of life from the house. The three beech trees shadowing the front shrubbery added to the general air of gloomy desolation.

Inevitably, despite the high spirits of her companions, she found herself speculating on what he was doing there, and whether he was alone now he had swopped the luxury of the hotel for the rather bleak and draughty grandeur of a house that had had armies of workmen tramping through it for the last six weeks and was still far from being fully refurbished.

It seemed a strange existence for a man who had the whole world in his grasp, who could buy what pleasures the need of the moment suggested, and who had no qualms about expressing his zest for sensual delights. Pagan allowed herself a moment to consider what he had meant by his cryptic remark about being dissatisfied with the décor, and she knew it was more than furnishing and decorating he had in mind.

It didn't seem likely that Michelle would welcome the new change of accommodation either, and Pagan was curious to know what had happened to her when the hotel suite had been vacated.

'Looking pensive,' observed Faynia, who had dropped in, with John in tow, on her way to a supper date with some friends in Ambleside. 'Not having second thoughts already, are you, sweetheart?'

Pagan gave her a half-hearted smile. 'Not about the crossing itself,' she said. 'I can't wait to get started.' She looked round cynically. 'Get away from all these damn people, shan't I?'

Faynia pretended to be hurt, but Tony interrupted. 'It's a cinch,' he said. 'All you do is get out to the Eddystone and turn right!'

Pagan laughed despite herself.

'I tell you one thing,' the young instructor went on, 'I wouldn't mind coming with you. Have you room for one extra crew?'

'There's bags of room,' she replied. 'It's the sort of boat that normally needs a crew of four. But it's going to be strictly single-handed.'

He pulled a face of disappointment. 'If you change your mind at the last minute let me be first in line. I gather Bobby's jostling for a ride too but you need somebody with a bit more experience than him——' he paused.

Pagan didn't react to the guffaws of a man standing at the bar who had evidently overheard Tony's remarks.

Hastily Tony added, 'I've got a good selection of charts given me by my father. Can't I bribe you with those?'

'I don't think so,' Pagan tried to laugh. Her heart, however, gave a sickening lurch. She had been bribed once that day, and the thought of it stuck in her mind and would not be dislodged.

Tim was waxing philosophical by now and she heard him telling someone, in defence of her crazy ambition she guessed, that 'the only way to be happy is to do fully what you're destined for.'

Shakily she raised her glass to her lips to drain it. What was she destined for? To barter herself for the transient fame of being a transatlantic yachtswoman? To make herself the victim of a man for whom she was nothing but another name in his long list of conquests?

As unobtrusively as possible she began to make her way towards the door. Now she had given them all an excuse to let their hair down mid-week she reckoned she was dispensable. If anyone stopped her she would plead a headache.

Coward, she thought, now you're going to go home alone to mope through the night. You got yourself into this mess, you'll just have to get yourself out of it. But there was no way out, as she well knew. It had become a question of going through with something that she found thoroughly repugnant.

Blind hatred for Leale de Laszlo filled her heart as she stepped outside into the night, and, head bent, she hurried past the end of his drive, fearful lest the object of her hatred appear and give her greater cause for heartache.

Next day she had no word from him and, embroiled in introducing a new influx of pupils to the school, she had little time to ponder over the date of their next 'business meeting.' When he had left her he had told her that he would be getting his own people to draw up the necessary designs for the transformation of *Silver Lady* into an efficient racing vessel, and that he wanted to go over these with her before work started. Pagan expected it to be a week at least before they need meet. She hoped she had made it patently clear that if she never saw him again, never would be too soon. After this one meeting, and 'the maiden voyage', as he so cynically named it, there was no reason why their paths should ever cross again.

It was disturbing to her stoically won peace of mind, then, when, as she was helping one of her pupils to beach the training dinghy late that afternoon, Tony came grinning down to the water's edge.

'Message for you, ma'am!' he called, even before she had had time to wade out of the water. 'De Laszlo International have called a business meeting for seven-thirty this evening. A car will pick you up.'

'What?' She splashed up on to the shingle, leaving the pupil to struggle with the boat himself. 'Are you joking?'

'Mr de Laszlo came down himself,' he told her, obviously pleased to have rubbed shoulders with a famous name in international yachting circles. 'You were just disappearing round the headland at the time, so he decided not to wait.'

'Of course not, no doubt he would say his time is money,' she muttered darkly.

Tony looked puzzled. 'There's nothing up, is there?' he queried. 'He's not pulling out already is he?' For a moment he looked crestfallen.

'No, he won't pull out,' Pagan replied confidently, 'Not now. We shook hands on it.' She shrugged. 'What time did he say? Seven-thirty? And what if I have some prior engagement this evening? What then?'

'Perhaps he thinks if you're really serious about the race everything else will go to the wall.'

Pagan glanced across at him. 'I guess he'd have a right to assume that too, wouldn't he?'

She began to wheel the trolley down the shingle

towards the dinghy. 'Did he say what the "meeting" was about?' she asked over her shoulder, with an ironic emphasis on the word meeting. Better to be forewarned than caught unawares. 'It's surely too soon even for the supersonic Mr de Laszlo to have got the designs for the fitting out on paper yet.'

'He-didn't say.' Tony gave her a hand with the trolley while the novice sailor splashed about trying to get the dinghy safely into position.

'Well, we shall see, then, won't we?' Pagan gritted with a determined tilt to her chin. 'We shall see!'

Prompt on seven-thirty Pagan, from her hiding place in the kitchen, heard the purr of a car engine. She didn't have to go to the window to look out over the small gravelled space at the side of the house where a car could turn. With a sickening dread she knew he was here.

She hadn't bothered to change out of jeans and T-shirt, nor had she done more than run a comb through her hair. Even if she could trust him not to attempt collection until the due date, she thought ironically, she wasn't going to give him a scrap of encouragement. She waited until his knock at the door had died away, then she moved, deliberately unhurried, to answer it.

He seemed to fill the whole doorway with his bulk. This time he had on some well-fitting black drill jeans and a black silk shirt—not, she was faintly pleased to note, open to the waist as it would have been on most men of his magnificent physique, but subtly undone only to the third button. Just enough, she thought wryly, to give a tantalising glimpse of a smoothly bronzed neck and the hint of fair hair on his chest.

As always his hair was outrageously bright against the tan of his skin, and she noted that the sombreness of his clothes supplied an even more startling contrast.

For a moment neither of them spoke.

'Aren't you going to invite me in?' Leale asked eventually.

'I thought I was supposed to be picked up and taken to a business meeting?' she stalled.

'Why not here?' he countered. 'There are only a few things I want to go over before seeing the designers tomorrow.'

Pagan could think of no good reason, apart from the obvious one, not to invite him in, so she stepped back with an icy glance to allow him inside.

He seemed to dwarf her in the confined space of the entrance hall and, pivoting, she led him briskly through into the sitting-room. It was just then that the sun was setting, and for a moment he was stopped by the magnificence of the reddish-golden light that flooded the room. For a few minutes the whole lake was transformed to a sheet of molten gold, but even as they watched, the sun sank behind the purple bulk of Ben Ridding and in a moment the water had become a hazy twilit sheet of softest blue.

'Thanks for the evening show,' he turned after watching it in silence. 'What do you provide for an encore?'

Pagan blushed despite herself under the lazy scrutiny of his eyes, fully aware of the suggestiveness of his remark.

'That's it,' she retorted, tight-lipped. 'You don't need to give me credit for nature's handiwork.'

'Oh, I won't,' he answered giving her a slow glance. 'Credit where credit's due.'

She moved rapidly to the far side of the room. 'Shall we get on?'

'You have a nice place here,' Leale told her, ignoring her last remark. She watched stonily as he moved round the room, inspecting the pictures, running a finger over the Tahitian face mask Uncle Henry had brought back from one of his voyages, and even bending to scrutinise the titles on the small collection of records and cassettes in their rack by the bookshelf.

When there was nothing left to which he could direct

his curiosity, he sat down uninvited in the middle of the rattan three-seater and regarded her with a curious appraising sort of smile.

'I think we'll have some Mozart,' he flicked a cassette from the rack, and, without moving from his seat, dropped it on to the coffee table between them.

Obstinately she glared back at him, but when his glance, never wavering, held her own for what seemed like an eternity, she capitulated with a bored little shrug of the shoulders. If he wanted to play silly games of master and servant, let him. It wouldn't hurt to pander to him over something so trivial—after this meeting there would only be one more, she shuddered, then he would be out of her life for ever.

She moved over to the music centre and selected the appropriate setting. When the sounds of one of her favourite pieces of music filled the room with its elegant strains her anger was mollified somewhat, at least she couldn't fault his taste, but she couldn't restrain herself from saying, 'I thought this was supposed to be a business meeting, not a musical event.'

In reply Leale drew her attention to the slim black portfolio he carried and without more ado opened it and drew forth the contents. With surprise she saw that he had taken the trouble to make copious notes on the basis of his inspection of the boat the previous day, as well as filling several columns of figures.

'You have been doing your homework,' she murmured, ironically.

'I hope you have too,' he told her crisply, 'You're not intending to *cruise* across, are you?'

'I shall race every inch of the way,' she told him, sparking up. 'I know there's no reasonable hope of winning the whole damned thing, but I think I stand a very good chance of winning one of the handicap awards.'

'That's what I think too,' he told her. 'I just don't want you to run away with the idea that it's going to be easy.' He fixed her with a stern gaze. 'The sea's a treacherous force at any time, and alone in a small sailing boat you're going to have to be one hundred per cent alert. You can fill your boat with charts and pilot books and still be taken unawares by a freak squall, a bank of dense fog, a sudden calm or dangers such as icebergs——'

'I'm taking the Azores route,' she told him, pointedly ignoring his little homily to the dangers of the project.

Leale looked up quickly. For a moment she thought he was going to start an argument about the best route to take, for there were equally good reasons, she knew, for taking the more northern route up near the Arctic Circle. It was generally considered a little faster, though not necessarily so, for she had heard of yachts being fogbound for days off the coast of Greenland.

'Why?' was all he said.

'I don't relish the thought of sitting in an icy fog for days on end waiting for an iceberg to come looming down on top of me,' she told him firmly.

'You'd rather waste precious racing time lying on deck getting a suntan, would you?' he asked drily.

'If it's a choice of either/or—yes,' she told him with a lift of her head. 'But I don't intend to sit around anywhere. I intend to race.'

'Nobody can help being becalmed,' he replied. 'It happens to the best of us.'

'What do you know about it?' she demanded scornfully. 'I always thought you people with your luxury yachts had power aboard to get you out of any difficulties.'

He didn't answer, but instead turned back to his notes and started to give her a rundown of the sort of equipment he wanted her to carry on board.

As he spoke Pagan became more and more silent. When she had first contemplated entering the race, it had been in the expectation that she would be one of the many under-sponsored ordinary little craft which got to the other side through the sheer skill and guts of the captain rather than by virtue of having the best and fastest boat, but now she could see that she was going to have every technical aid available, and the very finest equipment at that.

True, *Silver Lady* had been just a very graceful shell when she had first seen her, and any prospective sponsor would have had to fit her out somehow, but, she realised, now that de Laszlo International were involved the yacht would be transformed into a very high-powered competitor indeed.

With a tilt of her chin she jeered, 'You seem very willing to risk a lot of time and money on this project. Aren't you worried that I'll let you down at the last minute?'

'Through nerves or incompetence?' Leale asked at once.

'Either one or both,' she came back. 'After all, I am a—' she paused, 'female.'

'I don't see that nerves or incompetence are the prerogatives of females,' he replied easily. 'And I'm sure you don't. If you were a coward you wouldn't have got this far, and if I thought you were incompetent, I wouldn't be sitting here now. But of course,' he added with a grim smile, 'we shall see, shan't we?' Pagan raised her head. 'When *Silver Lady* has her sea trials and you have to face your qualifying test.'

For a moment she thought he was referring to something else, then she realised that he did indeed mean the qualifying test, the one that all competitors had to pass before being allowed to enter the race. It had never occurred to her that she need give it a second's thought. She returned his smile without a flicker of emotion. 'Let's hope your faith in me is justified. Or is this merely a cat-and-mouse ploy with the Inland Revenue?'

Leale laughed out loud at this. 'Do you really want to bother yourself with the financial side? I'd have thought you were going to have enough problems getting that tub across in something like a decent time as it is. My function is to take over as many problems as I can to leave you free to concentrate on the important bit.'

'Very well,' she replied, 'as long as you know what you're doing.'

'I generally do,' he whipped back. 'Let's hope we can say the same about you when you're in a Force Ten in mid-ocean.'

'If *Silver Lady* is going to be stuffed full of all the mechanical toys you've mentioned so far,' she retorted, 'I'm not going to need to do anything at all. I shan't even have to stir from my bunk. All I'll need is a good supply of magazines, and if I do get into difficulties I'll only need to whisper "Mayday" before finding myself back safe and sound on dry land!'

'If you do get into difficulties I shan't expect you to whisper anything at all,' said Leale with a grin. 'I'll expect you to drown like a gentleman.'

Mocking as ever, his eyes gave nothing away, and Pagan shuddered. The unexpected show of steel, even if it was partly in fun, sent icy fingers up and down her spine. His unpredictable toughness was a side of him only faintly hinted at in their previous encounters, but it had always been there, like something as yet unexplored, as if some time soon it would fully reveal itself without adornment.

She shuddered again. She could just about cope with his sexual bantering and if she kept fixed in her mind only an image of his emotional detachment, she could survive the so-called maiden voyage. But his icy coldness, the hint of what seemed to be an almost brutally callous disregard for her life was an altogether different game.

It was but slowly that she was training herself to accept, despite the pain it brought, Leale's indifference to her on an emotional level, but indifference at a time of real, mortal danger filled her with uncontrollable dread.

Her whole body had stiffened and she gazed at him with eyes suddenly widening with horror at the prospect of a watery and unmourned death.

'Pagan,' he searched her face, 'you've suddenly gone so pale. Are you all right?'

Slowly she fought to bring her fear under control.

'Pagan!' he said again more urgently. ·

She shook herself. Anger flooded her body. If she was less than nothing to him, at least she knew where she stood.

'Don't worry,' she told him in a voice like cracked ice. 'I wouldn't dream of showing up the de Laszlo name by calling for help, whatever the circumstances. I'd rather go down with the ship!'

He chuckled.

'Good. Then we'd better make sure it's adequately monitored all the way—for salvage purposes.'

'You!' she choked, unable to restrain herself. 'You wouldn't give a damn, would you? So long as your capital investment is safe!'

He gave another deep chuckle. 'I learned my lesson from my father,' he told her, 'property before people.'

'If you're anything to be believed, as a professional gambler, he didn't have much of either!'

'I wouldn't say that——' Leale paused. 'He died on a winning streak—a very winning streak.'

He sat back languidly and looked at her through narrowed eyes. 'But I'm no gambler when it comes to people or property,' he told her. 'I like to be in control of destiny as far as possible. The unexpected plays far too big a hand in one's life as it is.'

'Well,' she retorted, 'you claim to like a challenge, so you shouldn't complain about that.'

His eyes jetted silver sparks. 'You're quite a challenge, Pagan, and am I complaining about you?'

'I shall try not to give you any cause either. Now, is this all we have to discuss? I have to go out.'

It was a lie. She'd planned on an early night. But seeing him lolling there with such an air of vibrantly masculine ease was more than she could bear.

'I think we've just about covered everything,' he informed her after a brief pause. He began to stuff the papers together, back inside the portfolio. He shot her a look. 'I'd hate to feel I was keeping the faithful swain waiting—whoever's turn it is tonight.' He snapped the lock on the portfolio.

'Good,' she clipped. 'Then if you'll excuse me?'

She rose in order to hurry him out. But, irritatingly, he found some excuse to unfasten his case again. 'You might like this photo-copy of what we've agreed so far. I may have to ring you if the design team comes up with anything different. O.K.? Keep it safe.'

He held out the papers, already neatly clipped together, so that she had to cross the carefully preserved space between them. When she held out her hand their fingers touched briefly and he seemed to tower over her. She tried without success to avoid his glance. Any words she might have been able to utter died in her throat and she felt her breathing deepen as if she'd been running.

Without a word Leale pulled her into his arms, and, oblivious to the fact that the photo-copies were being crushed between them, he ran his hands expertly down her back, moulding her unresisting body to his own. Before she could stop herself Pagan had lifted her lips and with a drowning sensation she felt his own come down in hot pursuit.

Almost at once he abruptly released her. She stumbled back in surprise and the photo-copies fell unheeded to the floor.

'I never demand pre-payment, unless I suspect an intention to default,' he told her coolly. 'I'll see myself out.'

She heard the door snick shut behind him before her dazed senses had returned to normal. Then shoots of rage began to dart up and down her body. She clenched her fists impotently.

The swine! The heel! The—she could think of no word bad enough to describe him.

How abominable to be treated like this! She was thrown into a maelstrom of confusion. Leale was deliberately playing with her, treating her like a piece of fruit to be plucked when ripe. But she wasn't going to wait to be taken, was she?

She bent to pick up the crumpled photo-copy, hot tears stinging her eyes.

There was no choice. Miserably she fought the feeling of hopelessness that overtook her. Leale had the power to call the shots in this particular game. But afterwards, she resolved fervently, when she had made the crossing and her name was in all the papers—then, then she herself would be free to call the tune.

Only of course by that time, she thought with a hollow feeling in the pit of her stomach, there would no longer be any connection between them other than the bitter memory of the high price she had had to pay.

Hardly able to bear the prospect of the solitary hours before bedtime, she waited as long as she could until the sound of his car had died away, then, flinging on a light cardigan, she set foot outside. She didn't know where she was going to, but anything was better than staying in the house, yet she shrank from the thought of meeting anyone, so demeaned did she feel by the situation she found herself in.

It was in a state of such turmoil that she decided to walk, letting her steps lead her wherever they wanted. It's all one where I go, now, she thought, so long as I'm not in the house where he's been, so long as I don't have to talk to anyone, so long as I don't have to think.

She walked for something like an hour, up on to the fells that cupped the lake, and she managed to still her thoughts a little, to restore some vestige of inner calm to her ragged emotions.

Eventually, when it was almost dark, she let her steps lead back towards the lights ribboning along the main road by the shore. The walk had exhausted her, but at least the knots in her stomach were less painfully apparent.

Just as she came from out of the hill path on to the road near the pub, she couldn't help allowing her eyes to stray across the road to the now familiar façade of the manor. His car had gone. But even as she hurried past the entrance the front door flew open and a female figure, blonde hair streaming behind her hurried on to the gravelled drive. Pagan heard rather than saw the hurried footsteps which took the girl round a corner of the house.

The front door had remained wide open, but no one else came out. Pagan tightened her lips. No wonder Leale hadn't wanted a meeting in his office, flashed the thought. It would have brought business and pleasure too close together.

Head bent, she carried rapidly on home, past the gates of the shuttered house. Once inside with the door firmly closed behind her, it was all she could do not to weep at the sight of the cushion, still with a dent in it, where he had leant his head back to laugh mockingly up at her.

She didn't hear anything from Leale for several days, but one morning, just as she was leaving to do some early errands before the shops became too busy, the phone rang and intuitively she knew it was him.

'Good news,' he announced without saying who was calling. 'We've started work on *Silver Lady*. They're going to work night and day in order to get her ready for launching on the eighteenth. I thought it best to get things moving as quickly as possible, because the longer you have to get used to handling her the better.'

And, added Pagan to herself, the sooner you can collect. 'Fine,' she replied without a tremor. 'When will it be worth my while to go out there to have a look?'

'Leave it until the eighteenth,' he replied. 'There's nothing much you can do before she's finished. We'll go out together.'

'Yes, of course. We'll have to go together.' Before he could interrupt she went on, 'Will you yourself be down at the boatyard in the meantime to keep an eye on things?'

'I'm in Paris at the moment. And I doubt whether I'll get away before that date. But they're a reliable team, don't worry about a thing.'

Pagan heaved a sigh of relief. At least he wouldn't be able to come bothering her if he was away, and his words meant that he had the fullest confidence in his team too.

When she put the phone down she bemusedly registered the fact that that was the first time she had ever received an overseas call. He had mentioned his whereabouts so casually, as if nothing was more natural than to pick up the phone in Paris and dial a call to a little Lake District cottage.

Days sped by with no further communication. Several times Pagan was tempted to jump into her car on one of her afternoons off to take a look at the transformation being wrought on what was to be her home for the forty or fifty odd days of the crossing.

But the realisation that it was also to be the location of a humiliating transaction too made her superstitiously reluctant to set eyes on the boat.

Tim and Jan, in preparation for her absence, were taking a more active part in the day-to-day running of the school, otherwise, she knew, they would have sooner or later started to suggest a jaunt out to the yard.

It was reassuring that they were both taking such a close interest in the project, but excuses for her reluctance to take them over to view *Silver Lady* were something she wanted to avoid.

Tim, she was pleased to note, had returned almost to normal after his few days of euphoria over the coming baby, and Jan was bouncing with verve, in no way less efficient because of her condition.

Pagan had just washed her hair and was contemplating the possibility of drying it in the hot sun out on the terrace when she was startled by the high-pitched sound of a car outside in the lane. Driven at speed a sports car, roof rolled right back, shot through the gates and ground to a halt in a spray of gravel beside the back door. The driver's door flew open, and Michelle, in a white sun-dress and strappy high-heeled white sandals, flung herself out, slamming the door hard behind her.

When she saw Pagan standing in the garden she came teetering over the gravel towards her at once. Her face, Pagan noted, was fixed in a sullen mask, the mean little cupid's bow of her over-painted lips doing nothing to soften the hard-faced expression she was wearing.

When she reached the edge of the level paving that led round the side of the house to the garden she straightened up and fixed Pagan with a look of derision.

'I must talk with you!' she snorted. She looked Pagan up and down before bursting into peals of laughter. 'The wonderful *Pagan*,' she said and there was a wealth of insult in the way she said the name.

Pagan bristled but held her temper well under control.

'Did you want something?' she asked mildly.

'I'll say I want something,' drawled the blonde, the tight bodice of her sun-dress demonstrating what an effort it was for her to control her rage. 'I want you to stop playing this ridiculous game of heroines with Leale de Laszlo. He's wasted enough time on the project already, and a man with his responsibilities can't afford to waste time.'

'So he told me,' Pagan smiled faintly.

Michelle fixed her with an icy stare.

'I mean, about not wanting to waste time,' she explained, as coolly as she could. 'Although so far he hasn't said anything about time wasted on the Transatlantic. I presume,' she went on, still apparently calm, though her heart was going nineteen to the dozen, 'that by "this ridiculous game of heroines" you do mean my participation in the Transatlantic Yacht Race?'

The other girl's face flushed an angry red. 'You presume right!' she exploded. 'And just listen to me, sweetie—you're going to have to stop the game here!'

Carefully Pagan tied the pink towel round her wet hair before putting her head interrogatively to one side. 'I'm sorry,' she said, 'I don't understand.'

'Let me spell it out for you, darling, you're going to have to tell him now that you're backing out.'

'Oh, but I'm not—at least, I don't think so,' replied Pagan bringing a look of conscious surprise to her face. 'In fact,' she went on mendaciously, 'I'm rather looking forward to it.'

'You *are* mad!' exclaimed Michelle triumphantly. 'You must be to be serious about an idiotic escapade like this. You don't for one minute think Leale wants to go on with it do you? He got himself into it as a bit of a joke, now he's just trying to see how far you'll go. Surely you realise that? Any day now he expects you to call him to say you've changed your mind.' She gave Pagan an examining look. 'I suppose it's difficult for someone like you, living in the backwoods like this—' she swept the house and garden with a belittling gesture—'to imagine the vast interests Leale's group of companies control. And yet you seriously believe he'd waste his time with a cock-eyed twopenny-halfpenny project like yours? You really are mad!'

'But you seem to have forgotten one thing,' broke in Pagan, clenching her fists. 'There's the existence of the yacht he's having fitted out——'

The girl's tinkling laugh cut through the rest of her words.

'Of course there's the yacht,' she sniggered, 'what's so surprising about that? Naturally when you put him on to such a snip he couldn't resist. He's just a small boy. He collects yachts. Every businessman has his toys, and Leale's happen to be boats—among other things,' she added with a leer. 'But you don't seriously think you're going to get your greedy little hands on it, do you?' She burst into peals of laughter again. 'For one thing,' she went on, 'there'd be nothing in it for him. He doesn't need the services of amateurs. Not when he can afford something a little more up-market,' she swung her hips self-confidently, 'and for another, he's having that boat fitted out comfortably as a neat little two-berth love nest all ready to be sent out to Monte later this summer. Your best bet would be to save face now and tell him at once that you're opting out. Unless,' she added darkly, 'you want to wait and have him tell you himself when he gets bored with waiting for you to call his bluff?'

Pagan felt as if she had suddenly found herself balancing on top of a fifty-foot wave, with no way out but down. But before she allowed herself to slide under completely she heard herself saying, 'I don't believe you.' Nothing else could struggle past the constriction in her throat.

She felt, rather than saw, the other girl swagger towards her. When she focussed properly, she found she was looking into two eyes which were as coldly calculating as two cash registers.

'Your big mistake, if you don't mind accepting a little friendly advice, is to think you can hold on to a man like Leale de Laszlo by playing hard to get. He's got no need to wait for anyone—he can go right out and buy whatever he wants.'

'Some things can't be bought,' muttered Pagan, reverting to cliche in her state of shock.

'Well, believe me,' said Michelle, 'if a thing can't be bought, what use is it?'

'Some things have an intrinsic value,' began Pagan heatedly, struggling out of her numbed state long enough to come back at the other girl.

'Ha!' the sound was full of derision. 'He's a businessman. He knows the market value of everything—even of a self-styled girl heroine like yourself. And don't you forget it.'

'If that's how he thinks of people, I only feel sorrow for him,' Pagan returned, pride making her fight down the tears. 'I can't see that ultimately he's ever going to have much joy from anything. He might as well make love to his bank account and have done with it!'

At the word love, Michelle tossed her head and her eyes narrowed. 'Love, my little innocent, is a marketable commodity like everything else. Leale realises this, he's no exception. You'll learn.' She took a step back, swaying on the uneven paving. 'Anyway, now you know the score you can either take action or not, which ever grabs you.'

She turned with a flounce towards the low-slung sports car. When she reached it she paused and turned back, her eyes like two hard pebbles. 'At least you can't say you weren't warned,' she flung back.

Miserably Pagan wound and unwound the towel round her head as she watched the girl reverse out of the drive and go back, too fast, up the lane.

Her thoughts piled haphazardly one over the other like jumbled images in a slow motion dream. With all the life drained from her body, she made her way indoors. The sun outside seemed too harsh, too bright now. All she wanted was to hide herself in some dark corner away from everything that reminded her there was happiness in the world.

Is it true? Is it true? Pounded the question in her brain. Has he made a fool of me all along? But he said work was already in progress, so why would he start work on a yacht, spending time and money on it, if he had no intention of letting me sail it?

But Michelle had already told her the answer to that one—he was having it fitted out as a two-berth love nest. The vulgarity of the phrase shook from her a breath-stopping gasp.

Jerked into sudden action, she ran upstairs to the phone on her desk, quickly scanning the list of phone numbers pinned up on the wall beside it.

It took only a minute to get a call put through to the boatyard, and her voice was husky with emotion when she asked to speak to Mr Holton. In a moment she would know the truth.

'Hello, love,' came the genial tones when he was eventually brought from another part of the shed, 'and what can I do for you?'

Steadying her voice, Pagan said, 'I was just wondering how the fitting out of *Silver Lady* was progressing.'

She spoke as casually as she could, but even so there was a tremor in her voice.

'Champion,' was the immediate response, 'we're well on schedule.'

Biting her lip, she went on, 'I thought I might drive out to have a look at her——'

But her words were cut off at once. 'It's not that I want to keep you away, love, but I don't want to get on the wrong side of an organisation like your Mr Laszlo's—but the thing is, he did make a special point of saying he wanted nobody near till the eighteenth.' He paused. 'He wants to make it a special do, like, the launching, by the sound of it.'

Pagan's heart gave a lurch. 'That's all right,' she told him. 'I was just making a casual enquiry. By the way—' she went on, still maintaining a control over her voice, 'have the living quarters been fitted out yet?'

'Oh aye, he was most particular about that.'

'And the bunks?'

'One bunk he asked for.'

But before she could respond to the wave of relief that started to flood through her, he added, 'Double, according to plan.'

Pagan somehow or other thanked him and rang off.

Until the shadows began to lengthen across the bedroom floor she did nothing but sit staring into space, unaware of the passing time, unaware of anything but the anguish swelling inside her.

She thought she could train herself to bear the pain of knowing Leale cared nothing for her, that, despite the fervour of his kisses, she meant less than nothing to him. But to know that he had callously set her up as a figure of fun was impossible to bear.

As night drew on she crawled under the duvet, still half-clothed, but shivering like a whipped animal. Her hair had dried of its own accord long ago, but her skin felt first hot, then clammily cold as she stared unseeingly at the wall. Throughout the night she dozed fitfully, only to jerk suddenly awake at intervals until the first gleam of dawn began to sparkle the lake with the rays of the rising sun.

Wearily she rose from her place in the bed and made herself go downstairs to the kitchen. She had no plans, no strategy. In all her teeming thoughts had passed, fleetingly, the idea that perhaps Leale could be made to keep his promise, but she knew it would be hopeless. She would not want to exact an unwilling agreement, a debt, from him. And even if she had become a woman possessed by anger alone she remembered how he had in his professional canniness made it clear that their agreement was what he had cleverly called a gentleman's agreement. Nothing had been committed to paper.

From force of habit she made herself a cup of coffee without really knowing what she was doing, while the calendar on the kitchen wall mocked her with the black ring pencilled round the eighteenth.

Days passed in a sort of frozen nightmare while Pagan tried to bring herself to a decision.

Michelle was right. If she wanted to save face she would have to ring Leale soon and call the whole thing off.

But she could find nowhere the strength with which to do it. Inexorably she watched the eighteenth draw near. In all that time she half-hoped Leale would think better of his mean trick and call her with some trumped up excuse about having had second thoughts. But no word came from him, and she let the days dwindle away to a terrible few without being able to free herself from her state of limbo.

Then, two days before *Silver Lady*'s maiden voyage, came a call.

It was a woman claiming to be one of Mr de Laszlo's secretaries. She was calling from the London office.

'Unfortunately,' she said, 'Mr de Laszlo is in Indonesia and doesn't expect to be back before the twenty-fifth. Could you tell me if you will be able to handle the sea trials of *Silver Lady* unaided? A full written report will be expected by the London office as soon as possible after the eighteenth.'

Pagan gulped. It seemed there was no end to the man's satanic desire to humble her. Now he expected her to go through all the preliminaries, all the better to grind her ambitions in the dust.

Helplessly she told the secretary she would do as asked.

Half blinded by tears, she replaced the receiver. At least she would get a chance to sail a first-class racing yacht. If she made the most of her opportunity it would always stand her in good stead when and if she regained the heart to try again for the big race next time.

Numbly she managed to get through the remaining two days. Then a day that should have been one of joy and expectation dawned at last.

CHAPTER TEN

IT was bright, sunny weather, with a stiffish breeze and a skyscape of fluffy white clouds riding high in the summer blue.

It couldn't have been better, Pagan thought. It was a yet further twist of the knife.

Tim and Jan were both fully occupied at the school. She had made sure of that. 'It's not the launch proper,' she told them, 'just the trials. We'll have a proper launching party when she's finally ready.'

With a little glimmer of relief she told herself that at least Leale would be unable to collect his debt after all. Taking herself in hand was becoming a habit, and she told herself sternly that she must search out the bright side of things if she was to survive all this. What seems bad, she told herself, is often good, and vice versa. In some ways I'm very lucky, though it may not seem so.

At the end of the first day in which she took *Silver Lady* an experimental few miles out to sea, she was feeling even luckier. The boat was a joy to handle. With pain she had duly noted the fold-away double bunk bed, but everything else was as she had been told.

There was a slight worry about whether she could handle such a big boat by herself as the automatic rig equipment seemed to have been designed to be handled with two crew aboard, and she found herself wondering how well she would be able to furl, unfurl and reef the sails in a high sea unaided, just is if she was, in fact, going to race her.

She took *Silver Lady* out for two more days of trials, happier and with a self-confidence that came directly from experiencing the sea at first hand, then she ironically went through the charade of typing out a report. In it she kept strictly to the facts, giving no hint that she regarded the whole exercise as a farce. Indeed, her attitude to Leale de Laszlo was rapidly undergoing a sea-change as extreme as the change which had overtaken *Silver Lady* since she had come into the hands of de Laszlo International, and now Pagan was beginning to feel a cold contempt for a man who could play such an infantile and cold-blooded trick on anyone.

Her report had safely gone off and she continued to sail *Silver Lady* at every opportunity, so that almost a week slid by and she had still heard nothing from Leale.

It was after a particularly successful day when she had really been able to put *Silver Lady* through her paces that she was returning to port late in the afternoon. She noticed with a pang a group of men on the usually deserted harbour wall. The familiar bright fair hair and rugged physique of one of the men sent a shudder running through her.

So here it was at last—the moment she had been dreading.

She scanned the harbour wall for a glimpse of his companion, but she seemed to be nowhere in evidence.

Carefully, making clever use of the wind, Pagan allowed *Silver Lady* to glide swiftly into harbour, then, deftly, now well practised in the handling of the yacht, she brought her neatly alongside with a swoosh of falling canvas.

'Hi!' called Leale, detaching himself from the group in order to catch hold of the painter as she slid the steel-hulled craft gently into its mooring. 'Thanks for the report. It was most comprehensive.'

'Any time,' she replied coolly, ignoring his proffered hand as she jumped agilely down on to the landing. 'It's been entirely my privilege,' she told him, with a spirited lift to her chin.

He was wearing a bright yellow sailing jacket with a navy blue lining to match his navy blue oiled wool sweater. She even noticed that he was wearing professional-looking navy blue waterproof dungarees and yellow sailing boots. He even dresses the part, she thought scathingly as she gave him a quick once-over. The hawklike planes of his newly bronzed face remained impassive as he registered her look of appraisal.

'I'm sorry I missed the maiden voyage,' he murmured as they made their way towards the harbourmaster's office so that Pagan could officially check in her arrival. 'I did my damnedest to get back as close to the eighteenth as possible.

'I bet you did!' she shot back. He raised an eyebrow at the vehemence of her response.

'But no doubt the unplanned double bunk will not want for occupants in the future,' she told him bitingly.

'I certainly hope not,' he replied infuriatingly, giving her a wide smile.

Pagan had quickly checked in at the office and now they were standing in the doorway. The rest of the group Leale had brought with him were still in an admiring throng around the yacht.

'You look as if you've come dressed for sailing,' she threw at him as she turned to go.

'I hoped you'd feel like coming out in her again, to show me how she handles,' Leale explained.

'Just the two of us?'

'Yes?'

Pagan laughed hollowly. 'I'm not hanging around. I'm hungry and tired——'

He put out a hand to stop her moving off.

'Look, this is a special occasion, Pagan. I've brought champagne——'

The way in which she shook his hand off her arm made his words tail away.

'I'm tired. I've had a long day.' She began to back

off. There was something in his eyes which seemed to hold her and she knew the only way to be free was to go now before his old magnetism started to pull her back to him.

He barred her way. 'I want you to meet the designer. You've surely something to say to him?'

'I've nothing to say to anybody.' Her voice was beginning to sound strained.

'I want you to meet the other people who've been involved——'

'You want! You want! Well, I *don't* want! I'm going——'

Leale gripped hold of her by the shoulder as she tried to push past him, and she winced with the pain. His other hand came round her, dragging her up against him so that she could only kick ineffectually against his legs.

'Listen, granted you might be tired, but you don't have to be so damned awkward! You can stop five minutes and have a drink and say a few words to everyone. They've all worked terribly hard for you, and the least you can do is say hello.'

'Do you want me to scream and bring them all running? I'll meet them all right, if you don't take your filthy bullying hands off me!' She opened her mouth as if to put her threat into action.

He let her drop abruptly. There was a blank look on his face, but she couldn't tell whether it was astonishment or merely a cold anger.

'If you feel so strongly about it——' he waved one hand as if to show her the way out.

Pagan turned at the steps and looked back up at him. He hadn't moved.

'I suppose you wanted an audience in order to administer the *coup de grâce*? Tough luck! Sorry to have done you out of that little victory.' She felt her voice begin to waver, but the words poured forth uncontrollably. 'I suppost that's the last time I'll sail *Silver Lady*.

She's a beautiful boat—you don't deserve her. But thanks for the privilege. I mean that, incidentally. Thank you very very much. It's a wonderful little yacht.' Tears were pricking behind her eyelids. 'I hope you have many happy hours to look forward to,' she paused, and her lip curled with contempt, 'when you're berthed in Monte!'

Hurriedly she wiped damp hair away from her face to cover the tears which were beginning to stream down her cheeks.

Just then the harbourmaster came up and Pagan took the opportunity to slip away. Fearful that Leale would come after her, she almost ran across the yard to her car, and then she drove, fast, all the way back home, without stopping.

When she got in it was after six and the trees round the house were swishing angrily in the kind of sudden wind that often gets up after a day of sultry weather such as they had been having.

Exhausted, she flopped down by the sitting-room window with a drink in her hand just as the first large drops of rain began to fall. Distantly over the fells came the flash of fork lightning. In a few minutes the huge picture window was awash with rain. It blotted out the distant hills, and Pagan watched, half exulting in the unexpected ferocity of the storm, as wave after wave of rain was gusted across the garden and the lake turned a metallic grey flecked viciously with white.

For a long while she watched as the storm raged from hillside to hillside, and so noisy was the wind it sounded like a steam train as it rushed through the tops of the trees.

She didn't hear the sound of a car pulling up outside. It was only when she was startled by the sudden beam from a pair of powerful headlamps which cut a swathe of light through the gloom that she became aware of a visitor. Then there came a thunderous knocking at the door so that, suddenly tense with fear, she couldn't help but flee to answer its summons.

When she lifted the latch she stepped back with a small cry, for Leale was standing there, his hair, in the few yards from the car, plastered flat to his head by the storm. His expensive-looking raincoat had darkened and he seemed soaked from head to foot.

He pushed past her without a greeting. But once out of the rain he stopped. 'Sorry for the mess,' he grinned at her, dripping water all over the floor. 'Though you're in no doubt used to a bit of a storm by now.'

'Oh yes,' she breathed, regaining her voice, 'I'm used to storms.'

It was dark in the tiny entrance hall, but she could see his eyes gleaming at her out of the shadows. He shrugged off his coat, throwing it in a corner without a backward glance before coming directly towards her. His arms were round her before she could evade them, and she felt the old familiar surrender begin deep in the pit of her stomach. But this time she was not going to let it betray her. She jerked herself back with a snarl, one hand coming up to strike him hard across the face, while the other followed up with a rather less than effective punch under his chin.

Reeling more from surprise than from the actual strength of the blows, Leale fell back against the wall and with a cry of panic Pagan fled past him up the short flight of stairs. She had almost gained the sanctuary of her room with the key in its lock when, with a muffled curse, he threw himself after her.

In three bounds he was at the top of the stairs. They struggled wildly in the doorway of her bedroom, then suddenly she was scrabbling frantically on the floor by the bed with the full weight of his body on top of her.

'You little wildcat,' he cursed as she fought and kicked and bit him in a desperate attempt to escape. He pinned her whole body with his bulk, then held her jaw brutally with one hand. 'I told you I'd collect,' he murmured, fixing her with glittering eyes. 'An agreement is an agreement. You've had a week's grace, but now it's time to settle up.'

'I won't, I won't!' Pagan cried hoarsely, twisting her head frantically from side to side.

'Oh, but you will,' he told her, bringing his lips roughly down to cover hers. He jerked his head away before she could bite him again and tried to control her madly bucking form with the full pressure of both shoulders. 'You certainly live up to your name,' he murmured, nuzzling her ear in between random bouts of wrestling. 'You fight like a little pagan, but you've got to learn one thing. People must keep bargains. And you're going to pay, now!'

'You keep your side of it then,' she spat.

'I have done. You've got the boat, and now I want what you promised in return.'

'I've trialled it free of charge,' Pagan cried, 'what more do you want? Now just get out of my life!'

'You'll sail her across the Atlantic too, so help me!' he thundered.

'Oh yes, of course, I'll sail it all right,' she mocked, her lip curling, wondering just how long it would be before he admitted the truth.

'Good,' came the answer, 'so what are we arguing about?'

Her eyes widened in disbelief. 'When are you going to tell me the truth?' she almost screamed. 'You say you *want* me to sail it now?'

'Haven't I always?'

She gave him a speculative look. There was no telling what he was really thinking. But perhaps there was a way yet of coming out of it without losing face? She stopped her struggling for a moment. 'You do realise, don't you, that it's going to be difficult to handle that sail rig alone?' She tried to guess what was going through his mind, but without success. 'I'm going to get wet and tired clawing at the sails in a high sea with my bare hands.'

'It's bad seamanship to get wet,' he told her, but she flared up again at once.

'I know all that! But it's not my fault—it's the design—what fool decided on that?'

'This one,' he replied, kissing her neck, but with a firm grip deep in the tresses of her hair so that she couldn't do anything but endure it until he chose to stop. When he finally lifted his head, she was breathless.

Not to be deflected from what she had to say though, she muttered weakly, 'You should have known better——'

'I do. I did,' he murmured, his face muffled because his mouth was buried in the thick chestnut hair which had come loose from its clip.

'You mean you deliberately chose a design like that?' she cried, trying to bring her voice back to normal without success.

''fraid so,' he answered when he came up for air.

'Why? Why, in heaven's name? Why put difficulties in my way? It's going to be tough enough as it is. I can handle it single-handed in the sort of weather we had last week, but in mid-Atlantic——?'

'Too hard for you. Too difficult——' he murmured, letting his lips work their way provocatively down inside her blouse. Pagan tried to struggle into a sitting position, but he pulled her back under him.

'Leale, what do you mean? That I have to start looking round for a crew at this stage? Training them up? Or are you saying that you're asking me to back out altogether?' Her heart seemed to stop beating altogether as she waited for his reply.

'Stupid,' he said. 'I'm not letting you back out, and you won't win if you've got to train somebody at this stage——'

'I want to win!' Relief flooded through her.

Now that Leale seemed so adamant that she was indeed to sail his boat, she was automatically starting to think in terms of the race again, as of old. Time enough to work out why Michelle had paid her that dreadful visit.

'Isn't your bed a more comfortable place than the floor if we're going to discuss seamanship and allied topics?' He held her carefully but firmly in case she made a wrong move. Unable to resist the prospect of breaking free, she tried to jerk herself from under him, but he simply rolled back with a malicious grin. 'It's not that easy to get away from me,' he told her, nuzzling down inside her blouse again so that she could feel his tongue coaxing her body into a sweet surrender.

'No, no,' she whimpered. 'It's too cruel. It's too much. I don't deserve this.'

'You deserve everything——' he muttered, lifting his head for a brief instant.

'Oh, Leale, please don't——' she moaned. 'Why must you be so cruel to me——?'

'Why are you leading me on like this?' he demanded unjustly. He slid his hand underneath her shirt and his fingers were beginning to spread delicately to cup one of her breasts when there came a loud banging at the door. Then, transfixed, she heard the door fly open and the sound of a voice calling her name loudly from the hall.

'It's Tim!' She jerked her head up.

Leale's fingers still held her breast, but there was no force in them now. She managed to slip easily from under him and tried to straighten her clothes before stumbling towards the stairs.

'What is it, Tim?' she called down.

Turning briefly back to the man behind her, she ordered curtly, 'Stay in there out of sight.' Then she went out and closed the door on him. Time enough to explain away to Tim the car on the drive at some later date, but what could he want now?

She went down into the hall. Tim's face loomed pale and tense out of the dark.

'Don't you have any damned lights in this place?' he

cursed unwontedly, feeling along the wall for the switch.

Pagan clicked the hall light on. He was wearing his waterproofs and rain ran in rivulets all over the floor.

'It's little Ginny and the Robinson boy,' he said without preamble. 'They're missing.'

'What? Since when?' Pagan came forward, ice tracking her spine.

'René missed them when they didn't come in for their evening meal. Apparently she'd left them playing in the garden at the hotel where they're staying.'

'Surely they'll turn up sooner or later. They're probably sheltering from the storm.'

Tim took hold of her arm. 'There's more. One of the mirror dinghies was taken out after we all left this evening. It was washed up by the jetty of the Elm Bank Hotel half an hour ago.'

Pagan's heart gave a sickening plunge. 'Were the lifejackets disturbed at all?' she demanded.

'No one can get into the dormobile without a key.'

'So they've gone out in this without any sort of buoyancy aid? Those two know better than that!'

'There it is,' he shrugged, his eyes dull. 'This,' he said, indicating the still raging storm, 'sprang up an hour ago. They must have gone out when it was as flat as a millpond. The boat was driven on to the shore thirty minutes since——'

'All right, you don't have to spell it out! Have you called the rescue services?'

'That's the first thing I did. The second thing was to get down to the lake myself. Visibility is so bad just now it's impossible to see a thing.'

'We'd better take the launch out——'

'Pagan, love,' his voice was full of concern, 'even if they'd been wearing lifejackets they wouldn't last long in this.'

'We must do something!' Pagan's nerve snapped. 'What do you suggest? That we just sit meekly by waiting for the phone to ring?' She snatched up her oilskins and began to scramble into them. 'I suppose you did check that that mirror was ours?' she asked, clinging to a vestige of hope.

'One of ours is missing. They couldn't give me the registration number at the hotel, but I think there's little doubt.'

Pagan was at the door.

'Look,' Tim moved after her, 'it's madness to go out there now in this. What can you do? There's no point in risking yourself. It'll be like looking for a needle in a haystack!'

She whirled on him. 'You don't have to come if you're chicken! I'll go alone——'

'Fear isn't in it. I'll come but——'

'No, you won't,' said a voice from the top of the stairs, and Leale came rapidly down into the pool of light. 'I'm going with her.'

He took her masterfully by the shoulder and pushed her towards the door. He turned to Tim, who had registered no surprise at seeing Leale de Laszlo coming out of the bedroom, Pagan noticed, and said curtly, 'Stay near the phone. If you hear anything, flash the house lights.'

He opened the front door and began to propel Pagan towards the car. Distantly she heard the front door close behind them, then the storm seemed to cut them off from all contact with the human, and they were battered by the full force of the elements.

Leale fumbled for his car keys at the same time opening the passenger door and thrusting Pagan brusquely inside. Rain drummed deafeningly on the roof, throwing them into a relationship of sudden intimacy.

'Well, any plan in mind?' he asked as soon as the car was speeding along the lane to the main road.

'I'll check the store first. If they have taken lifejackets, it might be worth taking the launch out.

But,' she sat hunched, 'as Tim says, it'll be like looking for a needle in a haystack.'

The minute Leale brought the car to a halt on the foreshore, Pagan was out of it and running across the gravel towards the store. She was panting with the exertion of having to force her way through the raging wind which whipped the breath from out of her mouth, and when she reached up to turn the handle of the Dormobile to see if by any chance if was unlocked, she was gasping for breath like a swimmer. Rain lashed against the sides of the van. Tug as she might, though, the doors of it were firmly locked—so there was no way the two children could have managed to get hold of a lifejacket each before setting sail.

She started to shiver uncontrollably. The lake, its friendly blue as if gone for ever, was a moaning cauldron of wind-frothed danger. Nothing could survive in it.

Without realising it she was crying hysterically in Leale's arms. He stroked her hair.

'It's not your fault, my darling,' she heard him say. 'Don't blame yourself.'

'I should have been there,' she cried against him. 'Tim should have been there. I shouldn't have left him in charge.'

'You know that's silly. You've got to be able to delegate. And it's not Tim's fault either, he's done his best. It's just one of those accidents that happen.' He gripped her tightly to him and she managed to find a source of comfort in his great gentleness.

Eventually she made him walk with her to the water's edge. Together they saw the lake warden's launch, its light very small and insubstantial in the distance as it swept from side to side of the lake, steadily and methodically.

'I think we should go back to the cottage,' Leale said at last.

Pagan glanced across the lake to where the lights blazed steadily from the sitting room windows.

'No,' she hesitated. 'I'll stay here a little while.'

'But you can do nothing, my love.'

'I know! I know!' she almost shouted. 'I just want to be alone. Leave me, please. Go back, make a drink—I'll be along soon.' She looked distractedly out across the lake. Already the wind seemed to be less violent and the sky seemed to have lightened minimally over by Ben Ridding. But a white wall of rain still beat down into the lake and the intermittent clap of thunder rolled distantly round the farthest hills.

'Go back,' she told him, her eyes large with grief. 'I'm not needed at the house just yet, am I?'

Leale looked uncertain.

'Please,' she almost shouted, 'just let me be alone!'

He shrugged. 'O.K. But don't go out in the launch by yourself. There's nothing you can do that the warden can't do better.'

She nodded. With relief she heard him scrunch back to the car. Then in a moment she was alone on the rain-lashed shore.

She remained there till she lost all sense of time, standing in the shallows, her shoulders hunched inside her storm jacket, the hood pulled up to keep the pelting rain off her head.

She tried to imagine how the two children had come back down to the lake. How they had managed to pull the mirror on its trolley into the water. It wouldn't have been difficult, for it was a light boat, fibre-glass built, ideal for children. With smiles of glee like a couple of adventurers the two would have piled on board and set sail across the bay.

Pagan gave a start. A thought had struck her like a thunderbolt. Surely——?

She gauged the wind. It was strong now, blowing down straight from the hills. She was familiar enough with the vagaries of the weather in this part of the world to know that the wind would have been coming straight from the shore before the storm. For anyone in a sailing dinghy it would have been a question of a simple beat before the wind to get them out into the middle of the lake. Then there came the island, blocking the mouth of the bay, then, beyond that, there would have been a stretch of calmer water, in the lee of the island. Once beyond the island it would have meant coming out again into the path of the wind and carrying on down the long bleak length of the lake.

She peered into the rain-drenched gloom, but she knew already that almost directly opposite the island, on the far shore, was the Elm Bank Hotel. It was out of sight now behind the tree-covered rock. The island was really nothing more than a rock, a landmark. She had seen herself, only recently, that there was nothing much there apart from a few scrubby trees and that one look out point in the middle. She hesitated. She had enjoyed the peace and tranquillity of the island . . . . To a child the place was a source of mystery and allure—a place with all the magic aura of the forbidden, where pirates and buried treasure beckoned.

With an exclamation Pagan turned to the launch. Then she stopped. The fuel was low now. She knew, Tim didn't refill the spare tank till Friday. Briskly she scanned the long line of covered boats. Selecting one for its stability and size, she made her way at a run towards it.

Now that the rain had stopped and the storm itself was reduced to the distant grumbling of thunder, the sky had cleared and, accompanied by a retinue of stars, a crescent moon shone brightly down. It illumined the sleeping forms of two chidren, huddled together under a makeshift shelter of gathered branches. Pagan had almost stumbled over them when, without even the aid of a torch to pierce the gloom, she had alighted on the island not half an hour ago.

Two innocent castaways, they were unaware of the furore their disappearance had caused back on the mainland. For a long moment Pagan stood looking down at them until one of them stirred.

'Wake up now—come on!' She shook the girl's shoulder and drowsily Ginny had snuggled up to her. 'Come on, now, wake up! Your mum will be worried sick!'

Ginny shot bolt upright. 'Where am I?' She gazed round with a puzzled frown, then memory came flooding back.

'The storm's gone!' she exclaimed. 'Come on, Mate Terry!' She shook her sleeping companion before shooting a guilty look at Pagan. 'I'm sorry we took the dinghy without permission, but we just couldn't resist it. And Mum wouldn't let us land on the island when we were supposed to be having our lessons.'

Terry sat up, rubbing his eyes.

'You're certainly going to have some explaining to do when we get back,' Pagan told them sternly. 'The rescue services have been called out. At this minute they're searching the lake for you.'

'Golly!' exclaimed Terry in awe. 'Are we going to get a walloping?'

Pagan hugged them both to her, relief, now that she saw they were both safe and sound, flooding over her.

'You deserve more than a walloping,' she told them, the catch in her voice belying her words.

'We only meant to come out to the island to have a quick look round before dinner, but then it got awfully windy——'

Ginny broke in. 'We didn't know whether to heave to or find a safe harbour,' she told Pagan. 'In the end it got a bit too rough, so we decided to run for port.'

Pagan smiled faintly. 'Yes, it has been a bit wet, but I'm glad to see you're both wearing waterproofs. And,' she added, 'what are these?'

The boy answered now. 'Lifejackets, of course,' he

replied innocently. 'We forgot to take them off after our lesson this afternoon and nobody seemed to notice.'

'We couldn't have come out if we hadn't had our lifejackets on,' added Ginny.

'No,' said Pagan wryly, 'that you couldn't.'

She pulled them both to their feet, and they walked about a little shakily. They followed her as meekly as two lost lambs to the inlet where she had tied the rescue dinghy. Then they both stopped and gawked. 'Where——?' asked Terry in astonishment.

Ginny tightened her grip on Pagan's hand. 'But we left the mirror tied to a stump just here——' She ran over to the place. 'I'm sure it was——' She looked round in bewilderment.

'My, you have had a lucky escape, then, haven't you? It looks as if the tree stump was wrenched away in the storm too. The mirror, I might add, was found some time ago, washed up on the shore near that hotel over there.' Pagan pointed out across the water to where the hotel lights glimmered out of the dark.

'Oh, dear me,' murmured Terry, biting his lip. 'We're really going to be in for it now!'

'Come on,' Pagan briskly jumped on board, 'let's get you back. You're a naughty pair, there's no mistake!'

It was a somewhat crestfallen pair of children who huddled in the bows of the boat as Pagan sailed them all back along the silver path laid down by the moon. She knew René would be overjoyed to have them back safe and sound, and a few minutes' uncertainty as to what was going to befall them on their arrival back at the hotel would not do them any harm.

The shore seemed deserted as she splashed down into the shallows to pull the boat up. Then she saw a brief flash of metal under the trees and a car door slammed.

Heavy footsteps hastened over the shingle. She felt herself caught up savagely in a man's powerful arms and her body was crushed in the fierce grip of a familiar hard, muscled frame.

'Pagan, my darling, my love, thank God you're safe!'
His lips touched her face lightly all over, affirming the
shape of eyes, forehead, cheeks and finally, searchingly,
her lips. He held her at arm's length to have a proper
look at her. 'My God, you looked so desperate, when I
came back and found the dinghy gone I thought you'd
done something crazy——' he paused. 'We'll have to
talk. But later, when we've got these two back to the
house. René's there with Tim now. They're obviously in
fine fettle.' He shot a wry glance in their direction. The
two children, as if eager to make amends for their
misbehaviour, were busily stowing the sails and coiling
the sheets in very seamanlike fashion. Leale and Pagan
trundled the boat up the beach for them, and with the
tarpaulin neatly clipped in place, they turned to go.

It was nearly dawn by the time the two rather pale-
faced children had been safely delivered to the
rapturous René and the search party for them had been
called off. Inevitably the cottage had seen a stream of
visitors, and everyone had been duly thanked and
supplied with hot drinks in Pagan's little kitchen.

At last only Leale remained. There was a moment's
silence while he regarded her solemnly from the other
side of the kitchen table, then he was round it and
folding her into his arms. 'If that's what it feels like
when you only disappear half an hour on a little pond,
what's it going to be like when you're in mid-Atlantic?'
He hugged her convulsively to him again.

Pagan felt a flicker of something like hope uncoiling
itself deep inside her.

'Leale?' Her voice was tentative when she raised her
face to his. Before his lips could come down again, she
asked in a small voice, 'Are you trying to say you care
about me a little bit?'

When he at last raised his lips from hers there was a
silence which spoke to her more eloquently than words.

He made her sit down beside him on the oak settle.

'Pagan,' he said, taking both her hands in his, 'I've

cared about you ever since I first set eyes on you. I thought it was so obvious. But you didn't seem to want to know. Perhaps it was my fault—perhaps I gave the wrong impression. But I know I want to spend the rest of my life with you. And,' he added with a smile, 'that means all of it, including that stretch of fifty odd days at sea you're planning.'

'You mean——?'

'I'm coming with you. Why else did I have the yacht designed to take a crew of two? If you want to make the crossing, you'll *have* to take me.'

'Am I arguing?' she murmured, wave after wave of relief flooding through her. Tears sprang into her eyes. 'Oh, Leale, I thought you'd gone for ever, that all you wanted me for was——'

He held her tenderly. 'I let so many things come between us, so many misunderstandings. But there's an end to all that now.'

She leaned against him, secure in the circle of his arms.

His eyes gleamed. 'I've got a lot of plans. Don't expect me to be easy to live with. But I'm giving up this life of jetting from one capital to another. I could never settle down for too long, but at last I've found somewhere to come back to.'

'And someone to come back to?' she asked guardedly.

'No. I want to take you with me wherever I go. And I think that's what you want too.'

'Yes, yes, I do!' replied Pagan, a blissful smile coming to her face.

'We can have this as our base, for when we feel like staying home. And we can run the sailing school together as a hobby——'

'Tim and Jan can take over when we're away——'

'And we can convert the stable block to provide accommodation for the pupils. What do you say?'

She nodded, too happy to reply.

It was some weeks later. Just as Faynia had predicted, Pagan had found an occasion on which to wear the blue dress and it set off the large diamond ring she was wearing to perfection. She looked radiant as, Leale close by her side, she turned now to hear what Faynia was saying.

'I suppose this is bon voyage with a vengeance.' She raised her glass to Pagan and Leale amid the hubbub of congratulations and goodbyes. 'I hope you have a smooth crossing, and many of them!'

John added his good wishes, and by the way he folded Faynia's arm into his own Pagan knew it wouldn't be long before wedding bells would be ringing for her friend too.

It was late by the time they managed to get away from the party, and they went down to the lake to have a last walk along the shore before their departure. The big race was just three days away and they were to have a quiet wedding the day before.

'It's going to be a real partnership, my darling,' murmured Leale. His eyes were brilliant, exacting a response from her as he said, 'And we're going to start by winning the Atlantic!'

'Yes, my darling, yes!' she whispered, too happy to say more. Then she looked mischievously up at him. 'But Leale, who's to be captain?'

He took her into his arms. 'There's no need to ask questions like that. You know the answer as well as I do!'

With that his lips came down on hers and she responded with all the joy of her being.

ENGLAND'S BEAUTIFUL LAKE DISTRICT

Serene lakes with such names as Derwent Water, Buttermere, Thirlmere and Bassenthwaite nestle at the foot of verdant slopes. Towering high above are craggy peaks of mauve gray rock. Unlike the gently undulating countryside of most of England, the Lake District is a wild and rugged place, filled with the magnificent bounty of nature. Situated in northwestern England, in the county of Cumbria, the Lake District is so small an area that a motorist can traverse it in a day; yet it contains England's largest national park, its biggest lakes, highest mountains (which are also the world's oldest) and more than enough territory to explore in a lifetime.

Besides the natural beauty, there are remnants of many periods of history here: the prehistoric stone circles at Castlerigg and Swinside; the stone mound or "cairn" at Dunmail Raise, said to be the burial mound of the last king of Cumbria; the old Roman forts near Ravenglass, Hardknott and Borrans; the roads that carried the Roman legions north to defend Britain from Scottish barbarians, still traveled between the quaint towns of Kendal, Penrith and Carlisle; the hillside ruins of ancient abbeys; and in villages, the restored medieval castles, which are now private homes.

It is little wonder that the area, with its natural beauty and fascinating history, has attracted many artists and writers. Beatrix Potter, the creator of Peter Rabbit, resided near Hawkshead. And the great nineteenth-century poet William Wordsworth lived most of his life among its hills. Surely when he wrote that "nature never did betray the heart that loved her," he was inspired by nothing other than England's beautiful Lake District!